35—

WHAT A BODY!

AN INNER SANCTUM MYSTERY

WHAT A BODY!

ALAN GREEN

SIMON AND SCHUSTER

NEW YORK

For LEE

ONE

PEOPLE nearly died laughing when they heard that Merlin Broadstone had been murdered. Not in years had so popular a killing taken place.

Children learned about it at breakfast and stopped gagging over their Broadstone Bran (which they were supposed to chew the Broadstone way: thirty chews to the mouthful) and cheered. Timid spouses, shivering from bed and groping for the radio to tune in the morning's Broadstone Breathers (bend and stretch, one and two, touch the carpet, reach for the ceiling) heard instead the happy bulletin that the Caliph of Calisthenics, the Dictator of Diet, had been bumped off. A whole nation, caught up in Broadstonism as it had once fallen prey to mah-jongg and to Coué, heard the news and seemed, in one great moment of sighing relief, to escape from the guilt that had kept it breathing deeply, showering icily, and dieting distastefully during the last two years of Merlin Broadstone's health-peddling life.

True, there were some to whom his passing was sad. These were his original followers, the genuine health faddists who, for forty years, had read his magazine, eaten his

1

food products, made best-sellers of such of his books as *Diet or Die; You, Too, Can Breathe;* and *Have Fun with Your Body.* These disciples numbered some three million; enough to have brought him a fortune over the years. But they were as nought compared to the vast populace which had suddenly and mysteriously caught the Broadstone fever in 1946.

Perhaps it was guilt about too much postwar dissipation. Perhaps it was the meat shortage with the resultant swing to starchy, fattening foods. Maybe it was the neurotic increase of liquor and tobacco consumption. Most of all, it could have been the Health Hour, Broadstone's own program, a hugely successful audience-participation show on which simple people described their complex ills, and on which Merlin Broadstone, in his amazingly deep and muscular voice, advised them how to live better—and gave away washing machines and floor model television sets to the contestants with the most interesting disorders. Whatever the reason, Broadstonism took hold in '46 and held on to a nation that seemed superstitiously afraid to break away. But two things were clear: first, that the iron grip of the fad was primarily the living personality of Broadstone himself; second that, while compulsively continuing to exercise and to diet, the American people were beginning to hate it.

Consequently, when on the morning of January 3, 1948, Broadstone was murdered, it was conservatively estimated that there were about fifty million muscle-sore, palette-deadened, de-alcoholized, and tobacco-hungry suspects, each one with a powerful motive.

Fortunately for the nerves of the police officers whose

2

duty it was to solve the murder (there seems to be a law against killing anybody, no matter how unpopular he may be), most of these fifty million could be ruled out on the grounds of lack of opportunity. The murder took place in a remote corner of the United States and only a comparative handful was in the vicinity. Moreover, it was committed at approximately 6:30 A.M. Eastern Standard Time, when most people were asleep.

Unfortunately for the nerves of these same police officers, it quickly became evident from the nature of the crime that, far from having a plethora of suspects, they had just about none at all. In fact it took them less than an hour to determine that, whereas Merlin Broadstone was thoroughly dead as the result of playing host to a .38-caliber bullet, it seemed extremely unlikely that any human being on God's green earth could possibly have shot him.

Not even his youngest niece, Sandra, who, in all her blond and frustrated beauty, had the best motive of anyone.

"What we're looking for," said a police officer named Hugo, "is a murderer who can walk on the surface of a body of water six feet deep while remaining invisible. What we are also looking for," he added, "is a murderer who would put pajamas on his victim after shooting him and walk through the walls of a locked room to do so."

This obviously well-spoken police officer made that statement about three hours after the murder. He made it to a group of not-at-all bored newsmen who were intensely aware that the American public had eagerly gobbled up the radio bulletins and was impatiently waiting to chew

3

the ultimate drop of juice out of every morsel of detailed news that would be fed to it.

That particular group of newsmen was in itself unique. There wasn't a single news journalist, not a crime reporter, not an experienced leg-man in the bunch. They were all special feature writers and Sunday paper Resort Section editors. And they all happened to be on the spot at the special invitation of Merlin Broadstone himself. They were there to cover the grand opening of Merlin Broadstone's new health resort, a hotel and beach and fabulous exercise-ground occupying all of an island in the Gulf of Mexico some twenty miles off St. Petersburg and named, after a nation-wide contest, Broadstone. The winner received fifty thousand dollars.

Broadstone, Florida, was two miles long and half a mile wide. For centuries it had been known only to sea gulls, to occasional fishing parties, and to romantic boating couples who would, from time to time, go ashore there and, as they rather ambiguously phrased it, stretch their legs a bit. Merlin Broadstone purchased the island in 1946, by which time he was variously reported to be worth any-thing from five to fifteen million dollars. He built a vast hotel on it, he improved its beaches, he carved bridle paths out of its half jungle. He gave no thought to such frivolities as golf or tennis but built instead handball courts, calis-thenic platforms, and cut down such trees as might interfere with the tossing of a medicine ball. He did all this with the certain sense that he would make a great deal of money out of the place. But that wasn't his chief motivation. He had always wanted to reign over a territory in which no meat could be eaten, no wine could be bibbed, no tobacco

4

could be set fire to, no wastrel could remain awake after eleven P.M. or no laggard stay abed after six-thirty in the morning. Here he would bark an order and every human being within earshot would touch his toes (his own toes). Here he would ring a bell after breakfast and each guest would retire to his own sparkling but spartan bathroom and remain there for fifteen minutes. No more and no less. Here, in an auditorium seating eight hundred, motion pictures carefully selected for propriety and uplift would be shown on those evenings when Merlin Broadstone was not delivering from its stage one of those love-your-body lectures in which cleanliness remained next to Godliness but in which, by some evangelical distortion, the order of their importance became reversed. Here, he knew that for three months each year he could count on a capacity crowd. For, even if the nation-wide fad collapsed, there were always those three million of the original faithful; and some of them were devout enough and wealthy enough to spend fifty dollars a day for this sort of thing.

The hotel itself, the Broadstone (Merlin Broadstone called it that without trying to see what better names a prize contest might produce) was eight stories high and built in the precise shape of an open square. Three sides of this square consisted, on all the upper floors, of rooms, each with a private bath. On each side, half the rooms faced outward, over jungle, beach, and Gulf; the other half faced inward on an open court which was itself two hundred feet square. Within this court the sun looked down on walks and gardens and a vast tiled swimming pool. On each floor of these three sides there was a corridor down the center and every room opened, inward or outward,

5

from this corridor. The fourth side of this hollow square was the auditorium, its entrance facing outward and, hence, the wall it presented inward on the court was perfectly blank from the swimming pool at its base to its roof eight stories above.

On the fourth floor of the Broadstone in Broadstone, Florida, was the room occupied by Merlin Broadstone. It was on the west side of the hotel and faced inward on the court. If one stood in that room looking out its French windows (as the police were fated to do for many a baffled hour) one saw on one's left the north side of the hotel with all its French windows; on one's right, the south side with still other French windows; and, directly opposite, the blank wall of the auditorium's rear. Letting one's eye run down that blank wall, it rested at last on the surface of the swimming pool, whose waters lapped the very face-bricks of the auditorium's base.

The grand opening took place on the first of January, and thus Merlin Broadstone postponed for one year the problem of getting his guests to bed at eleven o'clock on New Year's Eve. These guests were truly guests. That is, they didn't pay. For the first week—while carpenters still trimmed and fitted backstairs—the hotel was filled with those who had been invited and, in some cases, commanded to be present. Among the former were the press and certain influential Americans, many of whom had no particular interest in Broadstonism but on the other hand no desire to offend its founder in an election year. No one ever knew where votes might come from, and who could say but what a fellow would get into the Senate on a roughage and deep-breathing wave. Among the latter—those whose attendance was commanded—were the members of Merlin Broadstone's family.

"There is no health without love," Merlin Broadstone *always* said, "and no love without health." He would say this during his lectures and he usually illustrated the point with lantern slides—and, occasionally, live exhibits—of rippling-muscled young men and plumply vigorous young women clad in bits of leopard skin. By such illustrations, he conveyed to his audiences that he wasn't talking about the abstract kind of love one has for one's native land or for one's alma mater and which makes no particular demand on one's lungs, circulatory system, or sinews.

Despite this viewpoint, he had reached the age of sixty-two unmarried and, as far as anyone knew, unattached in any more casual sense. But he did have a family. They were the Hutches: his sister Hester, his brother-in-law Arthur, and their two children Joanna and Carl; and the Lockharts: his sister Martha and her daughter Sandra. They were all—the six of them—at Broadstone on the morning of Merlin Broadstone's death. They were all there the night before his death, too. And, for various reasons, it would be well to see what they were doing at about ten P.M. on the night of January 2nd; a time when they were still heirs apparent and had not yet become heirs in fact.

Take Joanna Hutch, for instance, as—to her continuing disappointment—few ever did. This niece of Merlin's was thirty-two years old and continuously engaged in a desperate struggle against the return of virginity. She had a lovely clear skin and a mind that was even clearer—in fact, it was swept clean. There was an unblemished placidity about both her complexion and her intellect: it was as

7

unlikely that the one would entertain a pimple as that the other could be marred by an idea. She was probably rather thin, but she was given to the wearing of soft, round-necked, slightly low-cut, billowing blouses and long, vast, and flowing skirts which gave her a deceptive appearance of pleasing plumpness. Several people who had touched her here and there, experimentally, had been astonished to discover that neither they nor she had felt a thing.

At ten o'clock on The Night Before she was walking down a moonlit path. Palms arched above her, the hotel loomed softly off to her left, and a man paced gravely next to her. Her arm was linked with his, her hand rested in his massive palm, and gently he was touching her fingers one by one, as if enumerating them. This would have astonished most of his colleagues in the United States Senate, where it was seriously doubted that he could count up to five.

Happy Ned Drumbow had been sent to Washington by his Southwestern constituents because there was no legal way in which he could be sent any farther. Six foot four inches tall, thin and stooped, he had the finest pair of black, beetling eyebrows that any man had ever raised in noncomprehension. He had a resonant voice which almost any other man would have employed for the expression of ideas.

"It's sure a lovely night," said Happy Ned, "for the Southeast."

"Yes, isn't it," said Joanna, daringly taking sides.

"Of course, if your uncle had bought *my* island, all the nights would have been like this. There wouldn't have been no rain like there may be here tomorrow for instance."

Joanna lifted her lovely complexion to the sky. "There's no ring around the moon. They say if there's no ring around the moon it won't rain."

"My island," went on Happy Ned, brushing aside these meteorogical profundities, "is nearly half again as big as this island and it wouldn't have cost your uncle hardly any more at all."

"Uncle Merlin's very rich, isn't he?"

"When I told him I'd fix it up tax-free he said it was a deal."

"Carl said once that Uncle Merlin had maybe ten million dollars."

"Down our way we don't go along with a man that welshes."

"I know," said Joanna, "you hang them. I saw it in a movie."

Happy Ned chuckled and a sleeping heron was startled upward into flight. "No. We shoot 'em for welshing. Hanging's for rustling. We can't abide rustling. Except the kind you're doing. I sure like the sound of a petticoat."

And that was about as romantic as Happy Ned Drumbow could be. It served, though.

At this same hour, Joanna's parents were in their Broadstone room. Hester Hutch was nearly six feet tall, weighed a hundred and eighty-five pounds, and would defy you to find another woman in her late fifties whose chest, expanded or unexpanded, could match her own. You wouldn't be able to. Obviously, seeing Hester thus, straining her slip like a duffel bag, and remembering Joanna's veiled frailty, one would know that the mother had passed

9

on no physical legacy to the daughter. Yet Joanna had not been born without maternal endowments. For at this moment Hester looked out the window and spoke to her husband behind her in the room.

"I think it will be nice tomorrow," she said. "There's no ring around the moon."

"I wish it would pour," said Arthur Hutch. And added thoughtfully, "For about two solid years."

Arthur was sitting in an overstuffed chair. Which made quite a total of overstuffing. Where his wife was muscular, Arthur was fat; even his fingers were thick and pudgy, and this was particularly noticeable at the moment because he had laid three fingers of his left hand onto his right wrist and, while slowly revolving a cigar in his mouth, was attentively taking his own pulse.

"Why do you want it to rain, dear?" Hester was puzzled.

"Because then maybe Merlin will call off some of his damned bending and stretching and heaving medicine balls at people."

"But that's good for you, Arthur."

"Listen, idiot pet, maybe it's good for people who have nothing but muscles on them. Your family, for instance. But, as I have often tried to convince the Bounding Broadstones, I come from a long line of normal human beings." Arthur paused momentarily and bent all his attention on his pulse. He thought he had detected a skipped beat. The crisis past, he continued. "I am ashamed to say that my grandmother never could lift a piano without straining her back. As for my grandfather, the only time he ever ran a foot-race against a horse, it tired him. We Hutches are more the intellectual type. *We think*. And I'd love to know

10

where the Broadstone interests would be right now if this particular thinking Hutch wasn't managing them."

Bending down, he removed his shoes and absently started to scratch his toes through his socks. He hesitated, his eyes widening. Then with a muffled cry of anguish he whipped off one sock, twisted his bare sole around, and stared at it with horror.

"Dear God," he moaned, "that this should happen to me, a Hutch! Look, Hester, look at this!" He was pointing to the area between his big toe and the next. "There's a crack in the skin; and it itches. I've got athlete's foot. And I'm the only person on this whole benighted island who isn't an athlete!"

"I'm sorry, dear," said Hester, "but maybe you're wrong. Like when that bump on your head didn't turn out to be a brain tumor. Remember?"

"What I want to remember," muttered Arthur, hopping awkwardly into the bathroom and beginning to search through the overflowing medicine cabinet, "is to try to finish up Merlin's tax estimates, and conclude his next broadcast contract, and check the payroll, and finish auditing his royalty statements early enough tomorrow so that I'll have a few minutes left over in which to murder him."

"Why, Arthur!"

He returned to the door of the bathroom. "You know, Madame Moron, that's a fascinating thought. How *would* you murder Merlin? I doubt you could strangle him because of his neck muscles. Shooting's no good unless you hit a vital spot. Do you happen to know if Merlin *has* a vital spot?"

"Arthur!"

11

"With a rhinocerous it's between the eyes. But rhinoseri are on the whole a weaker breed than Merlin's." He took the cigar from his mouth and flicked a bit of ash to the floor. "Perhaps he could be burned down."

He came back into the room and fished some slippers out from under the bed. Sitting on its edge, he groaningly put them on.

"That, of course, presents an interesting problem." He began to pace the floor, the cigar in his mouth, his right forefinger ruminatively rubbing the fatty skin below his right eye. "If you burn a man down is it murder and hence a capital offense, or is it merely arson and therefore punishable by only ten years' imprisonment?"

"Arthur, I wish you wouldn't talk like that. And to yourself, too."

"Naturally I talk to myself. Remember I am a Hutch among Broadstones." He took the cigar from his mouth and regarded her sorrowfully. "And than that, Madame Hercules, there is no greater loneliness."

There was one other Hutch. Carl, son of Hester and Arthur, younger brother of Joanna. Carl was just twenty-eight years old, short like his father, and well muscled like his mother. He would have been a tennis bum if he'd had a better backhand. Once he had gone to Yale; but not for long. Just long enough, in fact, to earn from his father the sobriquet "A Dolt from the Blue." All of his strength had gone into his wrists and forearms; there had been none left over for his face or mind. At this same hour he was sitting in a room, a girl's room; and in his hand was a

12

highball. Carl behaved as though there was nothing novel for him in this situation. And Carl was no actor.

The girl was more than nice-looking: she was downright pretty, especially in this dim light where the pancake make-up was really effective. She must have worked in the hotel, because her room was in the servants' quarters. Yet you couldn't say she was a waitress, because she wasn't wearing the olive-green dress all the Broadstone waitresses wore. Nor could you say she was a maid, because she wasn't wearing the terra-cotta dress all the Broadstone maids wore. In fact, if that's your method of identification, you couldn't say what she was, because she wasn't wearing any dress at all. A pity, too, for she had the kind of figure that does great things for a dress.

"You're silly," she was saying. "You couldn't do any of those things. You haven't any money."

"I will have," Carl said. "You wait and see. Sooner than you think, too."

"Yeah," she said. "You're some talker."

Which was nonsense, because among all the people on the island, Carl was probably the poorest conversationalist.

And once again, at this same hour, there is another of Merlin's family who should be looked in upon. Martha Lockhart was Merlin's other sister. Judged on her own merits, Martha would have seemed a woman of some bulk. But, as the sister of Merlin and Hester, she appeared almost demure and fragile. She was the youngest of the three and the only one among them with some beauty.

Once, indeed, she had been very lovely. As you looked at her, you felt that the recession of her beauty was due less to the ravages of age (she was still in her forties) than to the internal pressures of emotional disturbance. And then you would have wondered what could have disturbed her deeply enough to mark her; for Martha was one of those vague and flighty women whose heads are as soft as their hearts, and with a softness as impervious to impression as chrome-steel. There are people made of flint, there are others made of suet: you can't dent either of them.

Martha, at ten o'clock that night, was in her room. She was darning socks, vast socks, double-bottom socks, Merlin's socks. She was darning their toes. She always darned their toes; for Merlin, the athlete, *walked* like an athlete, his weight forward, his feet thrusting out. He would have considered it a mark of deepest shame to be one of those slovenly, potbellied fellows with a shambling gait that wore out heels.

Across from her sat a middle-aged man in a seersucker suit, an unlit pipe hanging in his teeth, a few sheets of white paper folded lengthwise in his hand. This was a Roger Beeley or Breeley; we'll never find out which, because we never meet him except here with Martha; and Martha—as she was vague about all things—was vague about his name. He was interviewing her, for presently he hoped to do a feature article for his newspaper syndicate, a sort of profile of Merlin.

"Well, how long," he asked, "have you done all these things for Mr. Broadstone?"

"Oh, I don't do anything for him—really."

"You live in the same house with him."

14

"Well, yes. He lets me."

"And you do his mending."

"But it would be awful if his things were all torn."

"And you see that his laundry is taken care of and make sure his meals are cooked right."

"Of course, somebody has to."

"All right then, how long have you done all this?"

"Always—ever since I was a girl."

"How about when you were married?"

"Yes. Then too. My husband and I lived near by and I used to come over and make sure things were taken care of."

"How did your husband like that?"

She lowered the sock into her lap and looked off over the writer's head.

"Not much, I guess, but then my husband didn't like Merlin."

"Why not?"

"I don't really know."

"Maybe it was because you were doing all those things for Mr. Broadstone."

"Oh, no, he couldn't have minded that. Everybody does things for Merlin."

"Why?"

She turned her palms up in simple explanation. "Because Merlin tells them to."

"Did your husband and Mr. Broadstone get along?"

"I don't know. You see, they never spoke to each other."

The writer pushed his hand through his hair in desperation. "Did they ever fight?"

"Oh, no. My husband was a very small man and he

15

wasn't well." She picked up the sock and started darning again. "My husband swore at Merlin once, only Merlin wasn't there."

"When was that?"

"The night my husband died. It was the last thing he ever said."

"Why did he swear at him?"

"I guess he was delirious. The fever from the pneumonia, you know."

"Well, look, I don't like to bring up painful memories, but I'm trying to see some of the human side of Mr. Broadstone. Now just what did your husband call him when he swore at him; it might be a clue to Mr. Broadstone's character. Do you remember?"

She nodded rapidly. "I remember exactly. It was fifteen years ago but I remember exactly what my husband said. He had been unconscious for quite a while and then he came to. And he said, 'Oh, darn that old Merlin Broadstone anyhow.' And then he died."

Mr. Beeley-Breeley shoved the papers back into his pocket. "Well, thanks," he said, rising.

"Not at all," said Martha. "You know the chief thing about Merlin is his exercising. Morning, noon, and night. He keeps himself in wonderful shape." She looked up over her glasses. "I wouldn't be surprised if he lived to be a hundred." And, as the writer bowed himself out of the room, her expression never changed.

The roof of the Broadstone Hotel was given over to sun-bathing and to exercise. Its surface was dotted with mats and deck chairs; around its edges were brick walls, high enough to afford even a standing nude essential protection from curious outside gaze. In the center of one of its sides was a large area for calisthenics; and, at one end of this, a slightly raised platform. This, Merlin used in leading those mid-matutinal muscular workouts known among Broad-stonites as "The Stretchings." The floor of this roof sloped gently toward its inner edge, where the wall, every twenty yards or so, was broken by the area of a single brick through which rain could pour off into the courtyard below.

At night, this roof—which covered all four sides of the quadrangular building—was an ideal spot for strolling romantic couples. Unfortunately, romantic couples weren't attracted to Broadstonism and, on this night at ten, this secluded, starlit expanse was pitifully going to waste. Certainly, there was nothing romantic about the one couple who gravely paced it now.

While this is a reflection on the couple, it is in no sense a criticism of that half of it which consisted of Sandra Lockhart. Sandra, daughter of Martha, was, at twenty-three, as romantic as anyone could wish. Her pageboy bob was very blond with a blondness accented by her firm, dark eyebrows. She moved with a dancer's grace and yet with a purposeful stride. Her hands were buried in the fullness of her skirt at either side so that she seemed to walk as a boy with hands thrust into pockets. Her head was down as though she were studying her slippers as they toed forward with every step. Even thus, partly bent in upon herself, you could see that her figure was notable. It was such a figure as could make the loose, brocade peasant blouse she wore seem like a tightly fitting sweater. Her voice was a soft contralto which deserved to fall on ears at least five feet ten inches from the ground and fixed to either side of a young and godlike head. However, as she spoke, all her voice was falling on was an unreceptive, ivory-colored hearing aid.

This device reposed in the left ear of what might have been a two-legged dormouse in a linen suit, but which was, actually, the short and plump and middle-aged body of a lawyer named Daniel Joyce. It was at least thirty years since Daniel Joyce had walked in moonlit solitude with a very beautiful girl without being conscious that the night air was chilly. Once, in the Wilsonian era, his blood would have pounded in such a situation; now it merely shrank timidly against the inner walls of his veins. To each of Sandra's thoughtful, graceful strides, Daniel took two breathless and mincing steps. He seemed to be running along in an effort to keep up with her.

So did his thoughts.

"But look what you'd be giving up," he said.

She didn't raise her eyes. "A mess of pottage can be the most beautiful thing in the world."

"What?" he asked. "I don't get it."

"I won't buy security with my mother."

"How about *her* security?"

"She's never had any."

"She's had a roof over her head and enough to eat. Isn't that security?"

"Not for birds," she said.

"But your mother isn't a bird," said Daniel with considerable assurance.

"I know, I know," said Sandra, "but she should be. She isn't too old to learn to fly."

18

"You're a very impractical young lady."

"But I've lived," she said. "Practical people never live."

He waggled his head.

"Daniel?"

"Yes, my dear."

"Do you think practical people live?"

"I know lots of practical people and they all seem alive to me."

"That proves it," said Sandra. "That question was a trap and you fell right into it." She shook her head sadly. "Poor Daniel. I wish I could help you out of your trap."

"I'm not in any trap."

"You don't even know it. You're pacing back and forth in the bottom of your trap and you don't even know there's a big world up above on the ground." Her next statement came with no change of voice or attitude, as if it were all part of what she had said before. "What do you think Uncle Merlin will say?"

"I don't know. There's nothing in it for him."

"But there is. It will set him free. Don't people like to be free of hatred?"

"Your mother doesn't hate Merlin."

"She would if she could think about it. She can't think because Uncle Merlin has her mind tied up. Daniel, you've seen the ropes, haven't you?"

"I can't honestly say I have."

"They're there, Daniel. Every time she sews a button on his shirt, they're there. When she tidies up his room they're like steel cables. It isn't nice to see one's mother in steel cables."

"Suppose Merlin refuses?"

"He can't. Oh, he can't refuse." These words were delivered without passion. Sandra kept walking as she said them. Hence Daniel was startled to see her face contorted with soundless crying.

"Now don't do that," he said in some alarm.

"It isn't right," she said, "it isn't right to see people crying. Don't look, Daniel, I don't like being naked."

Daniel Joyce peered around in some alarm. If anyone heard those words, he thought . . .

"Why are you afraid?" she said. "Why are you afraid of what someone else will think? You should be afraid that I'm unhappy. There's nothing more frightening than unhappiness, Daniel."

"All right," he said, "now relax. I'll talk to Merlin."

"But fast. Please, Daniel."

"Very well. As soon as I can." Then he added without real conviction, "Maybe he'll see it your way."

"He will," said Sandra. "Unless he's dead. Dead people can't see anything. And so many *are* dead."

They went on around the endless roof.

TWO

THE bells rang at six-thirty on the morning of January
3rd as they were meant to ring in every room every morning at Broadstone. These bells—not too cleverly concealed
from the eye, not at all concealed from the ear—were controlled by the switchboard operator. Six-thirty was when
you got up at Broadstone. Seven was when you entered
the dining room.

Seven-ten was when Arthur Hutch got worried.

Merlin Broadstone's table was in the very center of the
great eight-hundred-seat dining room—its kitchen so cleverly arranged that an order of bran could be rushed to the
most distant table in ninety seconds flat. You would have
waited the rest of your life for a *baba au rhum*.

Merlin Broadstone's table was set for eight, but only
six were there: Hester, aglow with the scientific satisfaction
of one who has seen a No Ring Around the Moon predic-
tion pan out into a perfect day; Arthur, with the vacant,
introverted air of one manfully nursing a secret athlete's
foot; Joanna, with the soft, smiling satisfaction of a girl
who has conquered a United States Senator and knows
there are still ninety-five to go; Carl, with the barely main-
tained aplomb of a man who perhaps is going to be all

21

right provided nobody serves him a poached egg; Martha, plucking at the tablecloth with what might have been the nervousness of hands unhappy when they did not hold a dustcloth or a darning needle; Sandra, casting a speculative, disturbed eye over the empty chair to her right—the chair where Daniel Joyce should have been sitting at that moment.

But it was the other empty chair that worried Arthur. Merlin had never been late before in his life.

He was, of course, later than they thought.

Near the door, the headwaiter glanced alternately from his wrist watch to the empty lobby. Arthur intercepted the swinging glance with a nod that meant never-mind-waiting-for-Mr.-Broadstone-start-the-serving. For the rest of the diners, Merlin's absence was momentarily obliterated in a heavy flurry of prunes.

Arthur, with attempted but unsuccessful nonchalance, pushed back his chair and headed for the lobby. For a fat man, he moved quickly and with firm purpose. He crossed to the registration desk, picked up a phone, and said, "Give me Mr. Broadstone's room." Then, covering the mouthpiece, he added to the gray-haired juvenile behind the desk, "Have you seen him this morning?"

"No, Mr. Hutch."

The elderly woman sorting reservation cards nodded nervously in worried confirmation.

"I'm sorry, there's no answer," the operator's voice said.

"This is Mr. Hutch," said Arthur. "How long have you been on duty?"

"Since six o'clock."

"Have you or any of the other girls had any calls to or

from that room?" While he waited he reached across the desk for the passkey already in the clerk's hand. "Thank you," he said and hung up.

"Shall I come with you, sir?"

"No—and forget about it. He's probably just overslept."

Arthur's anxious, rapid stride toward the elevators and the clerk's astonished eyebrows denied the faintest possibility of this conclusion.

"Four," said Arthur to the elevator boy and stepped back as Sandra sped in after him. "Where are you going?"

"With you."

Arthur shook his head but made no comment till the elevator's closing door left them alone in the fourth-floor hall.

"I think you ought to go back to the dining room." But as he said it, he accepted the fact that she was walking along the corridor with him.

"Something may have happened to Uncle Merlin," she said.

"That's no reason for your being here."

"I want to make sure."

They were at the door. Arthur knocked lightly. Then emphatically. He didn't wait very long, but put the passkey into the lock. A key resisted on the other side. He pushed his own key delicately. They could hear the inside key fall to the floor within the room. It took a full turn of Arthur's wrist to open the lock. As he pushed the door, Sandra slipped through ahead of him. By the time he had crossed to the body she was kneeling on the other side of it.

It was quite a body.

Not even the shapeless emerald pajamas could entirely

23

conceal its various perfections. There was the massive neck which could cradle a medicine ball and hurl it backwards for twenty yards. There were the legs that could pace four and a half miles an hour all day long across rough country. There was the jaw that could chew raw pineapple (exactly thirty times) into a juiceless pulp. There was the jutting nose that could detect the odor of spirits or the faint whiff of tobacco at a city block's distance on a windless night. There was the forehead that made up in breadth what it lacked in height, and the great mane of iron-gray hair that topped the six-foot-one, two-hundred-pound frame. There, indeed, was the perfect specimen of a middle-aged athlete. He had died in the pink of condition. He made a honey of a corpse.

He was lying flat on his back, seeming to stare at the ceiling. His feet pointed toward the French windows, his head toward the middle of the blue, linoleum-covered floor (carpets are dust gatherers). His feet were bare and his pajama legs gathered up toward his knees.

Arthur Hutch slipped his hand inside the loose pajama coat and slowly drew it out again. He swore quietly and fervently, as at the collapse of a seven-figure investment.

Sandra, on the other side of the body, said, "He's bleeding," and pointed to a tiny purple puddle which had crept from under the small of the back.

Hutch reached across and rolled the body toward himself. The back of the pajama coat was red-soaked. The blood on the floor showed purple against the blue linoleum. Hutch carefully lifted the bottom of the pajama coat and looked under it. Directly between the hip bones and into

24

the spine was a hole. Around its edges coagulation had already begun.

"Is that a bullet hole?" Sandra might have been a visitor to the tropics asking, "Is that a palm tree?"

"Yes." Hutch might have been a native who had seen a million of them. He rose from his squatting position and crossed to the bed table, where he picked up the telephone.

"Good morning, Mr. Broadstone," said the operator. "We've been trying . . ."

"This is Mr. Hutch. Get me the dock." He watched Sandra. She was looking down at Broadstone, not quite as matter-of-fact as she had been before. Something seemed to have disturbed her. Hutch was reasonably certain that it was not her uncle's death.

Someone at the dock answered.

"This is Mr. Hutch. Have any of the boats gone into town this morning? Good. See that none of them does. Nobody is to leave the island until I say so." He jiggled the hook, and this time called the mainland police. Even with speedboats they wouldn't be here for half an hour.

Hutch hung up and went to the French windows. They were partly opened, leaving about twenty inches of aperture between the edges. He stared down into the courtyard. The swimming pool stared blandly back at him. He sighted from the left past the right edge of the window, and then from the right past its left opening. From the swimming pool to the roof there was nothing across the court except a solid face of brick.

"Uncle Arthur." The disturbance that had been visible was now audible as well.

"Yes?" Arthur seemed impervious to disturbance; he continued his sour survey of the blank wall.

"When you lifted him up just then. Remember?"

"Well, what about it?"

"Did you happen to notice not seeing something?"

Slowly Arthur turned his back on the window. "That's a fascinating sentence." He worked his cigar around with his lips. "What did you think I noticed not seeing?"

"His pajamas. They weren't right. There was blood on them, but—would you pick up his body again?"

"Certainly not. We're not supposed to disturb it until the police get here. What are you talking about?"

"Well, why wasn't there a bullet hole in the pajamas?"

"Of course there was. There had to be."

"I know, Uncle Arthur. There had to be. But I'm certain there wasn't."

Hutch looked down at the body, his eyes half shut, trying to recall exactly what he had seen when he had rolled it over. Evidently what he finally remembered seeing startled him, for he knelt with surprising quickness and rolled the body partly over again. Wordlessly he looked at the back of the pajama coat which was long enough to fall eight or nine inches below the wound. Except for the blood which had flowed onto the green coat, it was unmarked.

Arthur carefully allowed the body to return to its original position and slowly stood up. With his hand he felt his own coat, pressed his finger on the small of his own back, satisfied himself that there was no way in which a bullet could have hit one of his lower vertebrae without ripping through his jacket.

Sandra, watching him, said, "You see?"

And Arthur answered, "I'll be damned."

"What would they have been trying to cover? Why would they have put his pajamas on after they shot him?" Sandra put a half-clenched hand to her chin, held a red fingernail between her teeth, and squinted in concentration.

Arthur looked at her narrowly. "Why they? What makes you think there was more than one of them?"

"Oh, you know, *they*. They make the taxes too high; they always talk after the curtain goes up. They shot him and put his pajamas on afterwards. Why would they do a thing like that?"

Arthur rolled his cigar in his mouth. "I guess we don't know, do we? Either of us?"

"I'm sure neither of us does, Uncle Arthur." She was looking at him with utter candor. "Now then," she said, as if that settled it, "it's easy to say he was shot through the window; because there's no other way with the door locked. But they couldn't put his pajamas on him through the window."

"A reasonable assumption. Nevertheless the pajamas are on him. And, clearly, they weren't on him when he was shot. So how did they get there?" He rubbed absently at the fat below his eye.

There was love in Sandra's giggle. "Uncle Arthur, you'd be wonderful."

"I am wonderful. Only nobody knows it but us. You and I are my entire public."

"I mean as a detective. Haven't you always wanted to be a detective?"

"Nonsense, my pet. Detectives are notoriously underpaid and moreover they have to go out in all kinds of

27

weather." He cocked his head at her. "However, I admit to a certain fascination with the pajamas. How did they get there? Why were they put there?"

"I don't think the 'why' is so hard," said Sandra. "It probably had to do with time. Everybody knows Merlin gets up at six-thirty. So maybe he was shot at some other time than that and the murderer wanted to make it look as if it was while he was still in his pajamas. The murderer wanted us to think it was earlier than it was. Which means it was later than it was."

"Uh-uh," said Arthur, "if it was later than it was, he would have had his clothes on and the murderer would have had to shoot him through his clothes, then take them off and put his pajamas on. In which case, there are clothes of his in the room with a bullet hole in them or some of his clothes are missing. This could be determined only by a search. And personally I detest looking for things. Let the police engage in such humdrum futility."

"Wait a minute," said Sandra. "Maybe Uncle Merlin was shot in the shower, which would have been later than when he had his pajamas on, and the murderer wants us to think it was before he took his shower while he was still wearing pajamas."

"That," said Arthur, "would require a wearying examination of his tub and shower curtain."

Sandra sped into the bathroom and returned in an instant. "Dry as a bone. Both of them. It was a lovely theory, though."

"Police work!" scoffed Arthur. "For this we pay our taxes." He snapped his fingers. "There is, however, one formality which I believe the police expect of us citizens."

28

He returned to the phone and asked for the desk. "Please see to it that nobody goes into the courtyard," he said. "Post bellboys to keep them out." Then he added, "Have them continue serving breakfast. And if anyone asks, Mr. Broadstone won't be down this morning. What's the name of that Congressman from Illinois? Yes. Bentley. Send a bellboy into the dining room and ask him to come up to Mr. Broadstone's room right away." He hung up and looked speculatively at Sandra.

"I won't ask you why," she said. "I know he used to be a doctor. He wouldn't have brought his private papers down here, would he?"

Arthur Hutch had long been able to handle Sandra's bridgeless conversation with ease. "No, Merlin kept all his papers in New York. What papers were you thinking of?"

"His will, of course. He couldn't have changed it last night even if anyone had asked him to, could he?"

"He could have written a new one. Did anyone ask him?"

"I don't know," said Sandra. "I hope not."

Arthur looked at the watch face on the inside of his wrist. It was exactly seven twenty-two. The police should arrive well before eight o'clock. He relaxed patiently.

Somebody knocked at the door. Sandra didn't even turn her head as Arthur went around the bed and opened it. He motioned the bellboy away and beckoned the Gentleman from Illinois into the room.

Except for the tiny fleck of scrambled egg on the trim left point of his mustache, Homer Bentley was every inch the Man of Distinction. His fifteen years of small-town medical practice had convinced his patients that they

29

should, while there was yet time, become his constituents instead. He looked with an expert's air at Merlin's body. If he had specialized in anything, this was it: he knew a corpse when he saw one.

Sandra and Arthur stood quietly aside while Bentley did small boy-scout tricks.

"He's dead, of course," said Arthur.

"Quite," said Bentley. "Heart attack?"

Sandra pointed her toe at the little pool which had seeped from the other side of the body.

"Oh. Ah," said Bentley. He rolled the body as Hutch had and let it down again. "This is bad," he said. "We'd better send for the police."

"That's done," said Arthur. "There's no need your missing the rest of your breakfast."

"That's all right," said Bentley. "What do you think happened?"

"Somebody shot him," said Arthur. "He didn't shoot himself."

"He wasn't brave enough," said Sandra. "Or kind enough, either."

Bentley tugged at his mustache. "This is going to be bad publicity." Then he looked quickly at Arthur and Sandra. "Did you just find him?"

"A little while ago," said Arthur. "But he was just like this. We didn't shoot him."

"Oh, I wasn't suggesting—"

"Why not?" said Arthur. "There's going to be plenty of suggesting pretty soon." He lowered himself into an easy chair. "Might as well be comfortable." His right

30

hand strayed to his left wrist and he cocked a thoughtful eye at the window while he absently took his pulse.

Carl Hutch was not long for the dining room that morning. In fact, no sooner had the prunes appeared than he gulped a faint apology and fled the table. He felt no affinity for food, and he was on the verge of ending his relationship with the liquor he had drunk some hours before. When he finally emerged from the Gentlemen's Lounge, he felt somewhat better, but too weak and too much in need of fresh air to notice such details as the hotel staff excitedly gossiping, several gentlemen of the press occupying the lobby phone booths, or his family strangely missing from their accustomed table in the dining room. He pushed open one of the doors on the north side of the hotel and stepped gratefully into the cool light of the Florida morning. It was just seven thirty-five. At seven-forty he found Daniel Joyce.

Carl had rounded the hotel, passing the auditorium on the eastern side. He was about to go on to the beach when he heard the weak and distant but frantic syllable:

"Hey!"

He looked around with watery, red-rimmed eyes. Even their poor condition didn't account for the absence of any visible caller.

"Hey!"

The auditorium doors were open and the sound seemed to come from them. Carl climbed the flat, library-like steps and peered in.

"Carl! Over here!" Joyce lay at the bottom of the grand

31

staircase, holding himself up on one elbow, his left leg doubled seemingly carelessly beneath him, a purple bruise on his left cheek.

"What's the matter, Mr. Joyce?"

"For God's sake don't stand there. I'm hurt. That's what's the matter. My leg must be broken. Do something."

Carl's reaction was instantaneous. He knew what to do in an emergency. He crossed the lobby to the box office and the phone within. When the hotel operator answered, he said, "This is Carl Hutch. Let me speak to my mother." Sandra answered the phone. "Sandy, I want to speak to Mother."

"She isn't feeling well. What's the matter?"

"I'm in the auditorium. Daniel Joyce is here and he says his leg is broken." He listened for a few moments and then hung up and returned to Joyce.

"Sandy is coming over. She said she'd bring some doctor or other."

"Why Sandra? Why not your father or your uncle? For God's sake, don't they know I'm dying of pain?"

"Look," said Carl, "I don't feel so good myself."

Joyce started to swear, then, realizing that this young man represented his only contact with civilization, stopped. "Who," he said through gritted teeth, "wears a green jacket?"

"Around here?"

"Of course around here."

"I don't know. Why?"

"Oh, never mind. Skip it." The idea of skipping produced a new spasm of pain. Joyce gave himself up to groans and Carl stood helplessly fishing through his pockets

32

until he found an almost empty pack of cigarettes. He lit one and took several nervous drags on it. He was absently looking at the angry bruise on Joyce's cheek—it was just the size a large fist would have made—when he noticed that the groans had stopped and that Joyce was watching him narrowly.

Carl shrugged. "So what? So I'm smoking. Uncle Merlin can't run my life every minute."

Joyce tensed into a new series of groans. Carl's cigarette was a crushed butt on the floor by the time Sandra and Bentley, a bellboy and a bath chair arrived.

The fact that Daniel Joyce was not immediately taken care of was no reflection on either the medical profession or the Congress of the United States. Congressmen do not carry splints around with them, or even ampules of morphine. There was very little that Bentley could do except aid the painful process of loading Joyce into the bath chair and helping him through the hotel service entrance, up a service elevator, and into his fourth-floor room. With futile mutterings about a doctor who would be there soon, he backed out of the room taking Carl with him to get what Sandra had called an "urgent message" from Joanna.

Sandra locked the door behind her and came quickly back to Joyce, where he groaned in the bath chair beside the open window.

"What did Uncle Merlin say?"

"What did Uncle Merlin say about what?"

"The will."

"Dear God," said Daniel Joyce. "Do I look like a man in any condition to carry on legal business? I haven't spoken to him and I may not be able to speak to him for weeks now. Where's that doctor? And how did that Congressman know a doctor was coming, anyway?"

"It's the police doctor," said Sandra. Joyce waited like a man who quite properly expected further information.

"Uncle Merlin's been shot. He's dead."

"Say that again."

"Why should I? You heard me."

"Is this some of your double talk?"

Sandra stared into his eyes. He stared back unblinkingly.

"You know it isn't."

"I *do* know, my dear? Tell me about it."

"He's on the floor of his room. Daniel?"

"What?"

"Uncle Merlin was a nudist, wasn't he?"

"How the hell would I know? He took sun baths nude, if that's what you mean."

"Who around here hated nudism?" She didn't wait for an answer. "Somebody hated it, Daniel. Somebody went into that room after he was shot and put his pajamas on him."

To say that this fascinated Daniel Joyce would be something of an understatement. His jaw was suddenly as limply disjointed as his leg. "What in God's name are you talking about?"

"I mean it, Daniel. There's a bullet hole in his back but there's none in his pajamas. Somebody put those pajamas on him after he was shot."

Daniel stared at her in bewilderment and then, mercifully, fainted dead away.

THREE

OF THE considerable party of police and technicians who landed on the island about eight that morning, the only one who need concern us is the lieutenant of detectives named Hugo—John Hugo. Within two minutes of his landing he saw Sandra and quietly determined that whatever turns the case might take, they would, in so far as he could control them, be turns in her direction. The first of that series of police interviews which belongs in the history of crime as "The Examination of Sandra Lockhart by Lt. John Hugo" took place in a secluded palm grove about fifty yeards from the hotel, at ten o'clock that morning.

Hugo, his arms folded thoughtfully, leaned against a palm tree and a favorable light made his thirty-four years seem not more than thirty-three to Sandra. He had dark, rather curly hair and the planes of his face were molded as if by a sculptor with powerful and kindly thumbs.

Sandra sat on a rustic, pine-wood bench before him, one arm thrown over its back, her head tilted up attentively. Her face was a golden tan under the almost improbable blondness of her pageboy bob. Her eyes were a shade of blue which would from then on make John Hugo consider the Gulf of Mexico a rather dirty gray.

The interview had not yet begun. In fact, John Hugo was trying to decide just how to begin it. Finally, with the cunning of a trained police officer, he said, "Tell me something about yourself."

"What is there?" said Sandra. "Call me a bereaved niece, if you want to miss the point. I am twenty-three," she continued, "and I live with my mother. My father is dead."

John nodded. Obviously this was what the police wanted to hear.

"Were you on good terms with your uncle?"

"I hated him."

"What had he done to you?" The question was snapped out. A less astute police officer would not have realized so instantly that somehow the uncle had been in the wrong.

"He made Mother unhappy. That was an awful thing to do to me. Mother wanted to get away from him, only she didn't know it."

"But you knew it," said John.

Sandra nodded rapidly. She was being understood. "I knew it, and I tried to arrange it. I tried to go on the stage when I finished ballet school. Only I couldn't get a job and Uncle Merlin got Mother to persuade me to dance for him."

"Dance for him?" What kind of bacchanalian rites were these?

"Yes, to illustrate his lectures. You know. The Body Beautiful. That sort of thing."

36

John Hugo nodded. He knew exactly what she meant and he was relieved. "What about the rest of your family? Did they hate him too?"

"No. They *liked* being kept. Mother and I—we were the rebels. Only Mother doesn't know she's a rebel. I haven't told her." She looked off across the palm tops. "Mother was terribly afraid of guns. So even if she could have killed him, it wouldn't have been that way."

"I know."

She studied him carefully. He really did know.

"How?" she asked.

"You just told me." If there were guile in this, it was not evident.

"Policemen don't usually talk the way you do, do they?"

"Witnesses don't usually look like you."

Their eyes held each other in level contemplation. Each seemed to know that quite a bit was being established for the future. Neither seemed to reject the establishment.

"Will you be staying here?" he asked. "I mean later, after all this is washed up?"

"I don't know. I haven't thought about it." And then, obviously thinking about it, "Not here. Not on the island. I hate this place. It's all him."

"Where else, then?"

"I don't know. There never has been any place except where he's been. Mother always had to be with him and I was with her. I was trying to change that. Through Daniel Joyce."

"How? What could he do?"

"He's—he was Uncle Merlin's lawyer."

"I know. I was just talking to him."

37

"Mother and I are in Uncle Merlin's will. He told us so all the time. I wanted Daniel to make a deal for us. Some cash now, enough for Mother to live on for a while until I was earning enough dancing. If he'd have done that, we'd have been willing to be cut out of his will. Mother *had* to get away from him."

"What did he say to that?"

"He never even heard of it. Daniel was going to talk to him today."

"So you're still in his will."

"Yes. We're all right now." She shook her head slowly. "Quite a motive, isn't it?"

"Cut it out," he said. "I know you didn't kill him." He shifted his weight against the palm trunk. "When you went into that room this morning, who opened the door?"

"Uncle Arthur. He had a passkey."

"Was the door locked?"

"Yes. Definitely. Uncle Merlin's key was on the inside. Uncle Arthur had to push it through first; we could hear it fall on the floor."

"Maybe the inside key was just hanging there. Maybe your Uncle Arthur pretended to have to push it all the way out. Maybe he pretended to have to turn his own key."

"You mustn't!" exclaimed Sandra. "You mustn't think it could be Uncle Arthur. Anyhow, I *saw* him turn his key. He wasn't pretending."

"I'm sorry," said John contritely. "Which of you went into the room first?"

"I did. Uncle Arthur was right behind me. We were very careful to leave things just the way they were. We didn't even touch the other key on the floor. We went right over to where Uncle Merlin was lying."

"How was he lying?"

"On his back. His feet were toward the window and maybe a foot away from it. He had on pajamas. His feet were bare. Why? You saw him."

"I wanted to be sure that when I did it was the same as when you did. You're sure that door was locked? You're sure you weren't being used as a witness to its being locked —when it really wasn't?"

"Uncle Arthur didn't want me as a witness. He tried to keep me from going with him. Anyhow, why Uncle Arthur?"

"No special reason. It was just that he was in a position to get a passkey."

"Anybody could have. The hotel must be full of passkeys."

He waggled his head, pushed away from the palm trunk, and came over to sit beside her on the bench. His eyes didn't shift from hers. Nor did she move her arm from where it lay along the top of the bench.

"We've been into that," he said. "The maids hadn't come on duty yet and all their keys were locked up in the housekeeper's room. The two watchmen have alibis and no reasonable motives. The only other passkey was at the desk, and two people swear it was there from the time they came on duty at six until your Uncle Arthur asked for it. And," he stretched out his legs, "the doctor assures us that Merlin Broadstone died not long before seven—we're assuming about a quarter of."

"You'd be closer," said Carl Hutch, stepping into the grove, "if you said twenty of."

"Oh," said John Hugo, "you've been listening in on this."

"Naturally."

"You bet," said Sandra to John, "very naturally."

"Why twenty of?" asked John.

"Because that's when I saw the gun go off."

"You might," said John, "tell me about it. I promise not to be bored."

"Well, it was like this." Now Carl was leaning against the palm trunk. It was a poor imitation. "I was standing at my window this morning looking into the court. My room's on the fourth floor across the corridor from Mother's and Dad's. On the north side of the hotel. While I was standing there I saw this flash come out of the swimming pool. Only I wasn't sure whether I'd really seen it or not."

"Why not?"

"Because I was plenty hung over. I was but stiff last night. I was at a little party."

John considered him. "I thought this place was dry."

Carl snorted. "It says here."

"How did you sneak in? I thought they locked up at eleven."

"I wasn't outside. I just wasn't in my room."

"Mind telling me whose room you were in?"

"Yes, I'd mind. I don't think it's important and I'd rather keep a nice girl out of this."

Sandra looked at him with evident skepticism.

"Skipping the identity of the lucky girl for a moment," said John, "what makes you so sure it was just twenty of seven, when you were too hung over to be sure it was a shot?"

"Because I looked at my watch. You see *then* I was sure

it was a shot and I figured I ought to see what time it was fired. Later I began to doubt the whole thing, I was feeling so awful."

"What else did you see in the swimming pool?"

"Nothing. And nobody. Just the shot coming out of it."

"But that's impossible, isn't it?" said Sandra to John. "A shot coming out of a swimming pool?"

"I'd say so. And on the other hand it seems as though it had to come from there."

He added nothing to that statement. Sandra watched him questioningly.

"Big secret, huh?" said Carl.

"Not especially. The doctor probed the bullet track. It went into the small of his back and ended up in his heart."

"So he was shot from below," said Carl.

"Yeah."

"Might have been someone lying on the floor of his room," Carl suggested.

"You'd be surprised," said Sandra, "how few people go around lying on floors."

"Whoever shot him wasn't in the room," said John. "A .38 makes more mess than that at short range. So the bullet had to come from outside. And the French windows were open only about a foot and a half and the glass wasn't broken. So the bullet had to come from straight across the way. And from down below. In fact, we plotted its line. The bullet that hit your uncle in the back had to come from where that blank wall meets the edge of the swimming pool. In other words—as a gun can't be fired with any accuracy from under water—it had to come from just above the surface of the water and from right up against the auditorium wall."

"Like someone floating?"

John shrugged.

"Or treading water?"

"Or lying on a raft. Or hanging by his fingernails to the wall. Or being under water and holding the gun out of it—although how you'd aim that way I don't know."

Carl suddenly changed the subject. "Was anything missing from the room? Something small and brown? His wallet maybe?"

"His wallet was in the room," said John. "What are you getting at?"

"I'm not sure," said Carl. "I'm not a damn bit sure about any of it. It's like the flash from the swimming pool. Only, so help me, it seems now that right after I saw that flash I saw something come out of a window. Like it was thrown. It was a window near where Merlin's was. Maybe it was even his window. Two things. It's the damnedest feeling. Two things coming out of a window. Small and brown." He straightened up, away from the palm trunk. "If I really saw them, they would be there yet, in the court. They went down into the court—into a clump of bushes."

"We could look," said Hugo.

They cut toward the hotel, into the lobby, and across it. A bellboy stood aside as Hugo led them into the courtyard.

The morning sun was high enough now to be shining directly into almost every part of the court. Palmettos bordered its paths, oleanders bloomed recklessly. Near the

42

pool, an artificial beach held umbrellas, beach chairs, and a few metal tables. It was still, almost windless, in the court. The swimming pool lapped quietly.

Carl looked upward toward the northern wall, as if trying to locate his own room, then turned and not too certainly moved toward a large oleander clump some thirty feet out from the western side.

They never got quite to it.

The oleander clump began to move. It shook. It trembled. It emitted a deep groan. Then it subsided and in its center stood Arthur Hutch, breathing heavily.

"Hah!" he said to them. Then he looked down at his hands and raised them above the level of the bush. "Who," he demanded, "would have thrown these out of Merlin's room? And why?"

They were certainly brown. But each of them was considerably larger than a wallet. Arthur Hutch was standing there holding Merlin Broadstone's bedroom slippers.

"There's just one thing I want to know, Mr. Hutch," Hugo said. "Where do you think you were at six-forty this morning?"

"Think I was, my eye! I was in the shower, and I was in there a good solid fifteen minutes."

"Quite sure of that?"

"Positive."

"Couldn't have been anywhere near your window around that time?"

"Unlike most of the family I married into, I bathe in private. No, I was nowhere near the window."

"You didn't see those slippers land in the bush, then?"

"Certainly not. Anyhow, my window faces the other way. Not on the court."

"Then how did you know they were there?"

"It occurred to me that they had to be. You see, I happen to know beyond a doubt that Merlin Broadstone wore slippers. He couldn't have gone around in bare feet. I have been studying the body and"—here he shook the slipper in his right hand at John Hugo's nose—"I can tell you one thing. Merlin Broadstone is not the guilty man."

"You mean he didn't kill himself?"

"I'm not talking of killing. I have been examining the body and one thing I can clear Broadstone of. He is not the man who gave me athlete's foot. But so help me when I lay my hands on the culprit—" Hutch gave a shudder which might have been at thought of the vengeance he would wreak, or might have been the result of his effort to climb out of the bush. "Here," he said, "take your evidence," and, tossing the slippers to Hugo, strode to the lobby. "Come along, Carl," he called over his shoulder. "There are things for us to do."

Hugo watched the father and son as they disappeared into the hotel. He looked down at the slippers and then at Sandra. "Neat," he said. "Very neat."

Sandra looked at him and put a hand in an almost restraining gesture on his arm. "Maybe there *are* things for them to do," she said.

"So?" said John.

"Maybe there are. Maybe he wasn't trying to get Carl out of here to talk to him before he said any more to you." She looked up at Merlin's window and then across the court to the swimming pool as if gauging the distance.

44

"I don't think so," she said. "You should have seen Carl at breakfast. He was really hung over. He couldn't even hold a spoon."

Clearly this satisfied Hugo. If Sandra said Carl couldn't hold a spoon, then Carl couldn't hold a spoon. And certainly that meant that he couldn't hold a gun. Such was the police lieutenant's sensitivity to Sandra that not for one moment did he ponder the rapidity with which she was ruling out suspects.

A middle-aged policeman whose shield hung crooked on his wrinkled blue shirt came out of the lobby door and crossed the courtyard to them.

"Lieutenant, there's a dame says she wants to put some socks away."

"Yes?" asked Hugo, who felt that there must be more to it than this.

"She wants to put them in the murdered guy's bureau. She says they belong there. I tried to tell her he wasn't going to need any more socks except one pair—black silk, you know. We haven't let her in the room, but she keeps hanging around outside it. I figured maybe you'd want to know."

"That's Mother," said Sandra. "She'd never let anyone else touch his socks."

"Tell her—no, wait a minute," said John. "We'll go up and see her. I am very anxious to meet—that is, I want to interview your mother."

In the fourth-floor corridor several policemen lounged near the entrance to Merlin's room. The doors of other rooms stood partly open, and the occupants, who clearly

45

had been ordered not to clutter up the hall, peered from their thresholds waiting to see what they could see—which was exactly nothing. The arrival of Sandra and Hugo created a small sensation. Hugo had no intention of interviewing Martha Lockhart in this atmosphere.

Martha, in a simple cotton house dress, holding a workbasket piled with socks, waited patiently at precisely that distance from Merlin's door which was obviously the closest point the guardian police had permitted her to reach.

"Mother," said Sandra, "I'd like you to meet Lieutenant Hugo. He and I have been chatting about the case. He is really quite interested in it and I am sure you will enjoy talking to him."

"How do you do, Mrs. Lockhart," said John. "I am very sorry about your brother. Is there anything I can do for you?"

Martha raised the basket a little bit. "These socks belong in his drawer. Merlin's terribly particular about them being back there every morning."

"I am sure that can be arranged. Just a moment." John stepped aside and muttered to one of the police, "They get him out of there yet?"

"Yeah, the medical examiner finished up half an hour ago."

"Photographs? Fingerprints?"

"Yeah, all done."

"Anybody cleaned up the floor?"

"I did it myself."

John turned to the two women. "Come right in, Mrs. Lockhart. We'll put those socks away." He held the door open for her. Martha hesitated on the threshold. It might have been a pause of compunction—or a momentary, appraising glance. Then she marched in. Sandra and John followed, and the door closed behind them.

John stood leaning against the back of the desk chair, his hands behind him resting on its top. Sandra half reclined, half sat on the foot of the bed, one leg swinging slowly in the sunlight which focused through the window. Both of them were quietly watching Martha Lockhart at the bureau. There was something sadly unhurried about her actions. She placed the basket on top of the bureau and drew an upper drawer out slowly. Her hands ran over the socks in the drawer as if feeling them into place. She didn't seem quite to be looking at them. With her back to John and Sandra, it wasn't easy for them to tell whether this was the sightlessness of one whose eyes were filled with tears. Then, one rolled-up pair at a time, she took the mended socks from her basket and placed them carefully into little nests that her hands made among the other socks. When she had finished, she closed the drawer with such slow solemnity that John could think of nothing except canvas straps slipping slowly through tensed hands and a coffin gradually lowering.

Then Martha opened the drawer below. From where he stood, John could see underwear and pajamas. Almost briskly now Martha rearranged this drawer—perhaps dwelling a little longer on the pile of pajamas than on the rest of its contents. She closed it and went to the bottom drawer, measured the careful alignment of the shirts within it, and closed it with a snap of finality.

It would have been hard to say whether all this were one last lingering look or one first cautious search.

Martha picked up the basket from the bureau top and

47

turned around. "I should have done this last night. Merlin always liked his things put back before he went to bed. Only he wouldn't let me in. It's the first time he ever wouldn't let me in."

"Sit down, Mrs. Lockhart," said John.

"Thank you." She went over to the easy chair and sat in it, stiffly upright and on its edge, using none of its cushioned depth. She might just as well have been sitting on a camp chair—the sort an undertaker brings for a little funeral at home.

"Why wouldn't he let you in?"

"He said he was busy when I knocked. Somebody was with him. I heard him talking to somebody just before I knocked."

"Do you remember what he was saying?"

"Yes. I heard him say, 'For vegetarians.' "

"Why do you think he said that?"

"Why not? He always said things like that."

"Who do you think he was talking to?"

"I don't know. Whoever it was must have said something because after a few seconds I heard Merlin say, 'No, no. Not rich Rotarians. Vegetarians.' "

"What time was that?" said John.

"It would have been almost exactly twenty of eleven."

"How can you be so sure?"

"Well, a man was interviewing me last night about Merlin. A writer. And when he left I tuned in the ten-thirty sports broadcast to get the race results from Santa Anita."

"Oh, really?" said John, as if struggling to accept a new facet of Martha's character. "Are you interested in horse racing?"

48

"Oh, no. I've never been to one."

Sandra's foot stopped swinging. "My father was very fond of horse racing and he always tuned in the race results at night. Mother does it in memory of him."

John nodded sympathetically. Obviously this was the most touching trait he had ever heard of. "So as soon as you heard the—the race results, you came along to put the socks away?"

"That's right," said Martha. "That's the time almost every night that I come to Merlin's room to make sure everything is taken care of, and to turn his bed back. That's when we'd talk. He would always be in his pajamas so that as soon as I left he could go to bed. But first we'd talk. Last night was the first time I ever couldn't get in." Now there were undoubtedly tears in her eyes. John felt that this may not have been a sister's grief so much as any woman's hurt feelings.

"It was before you knocked on the door that you heard your brother say those things?"

"Yes."

"When you did knock on the door, what happened?"

"He said, 'Not now. Not tonight. I don't want to be disturbed.'"

"Do you think he knew it was you?"

"Of course he did," said Martha. "Who else would it have been?"

"Then what happened?"

"I started back to my room."

"Did you hear him say anything else?"

"Yes, he did say something else. Only I can't remember it now—and I thought it was funny last night. He sounded like that Senator."

49

John leaned forward. "You mean Senator Drumbow? The one who's staying here?"

"No, that Senator on the radio. You know, that one on Sunday nights, Sandra."

Sandra explained to John. "Mother means the one on Fred Allen's program. Senator Claghorne. You know."

"Now let's get this straight," said John. "Just before you left this door you heard Merlin Broadstone say something that made him sound like Senator Claghorne."

"Yes," said Martha.

"Well, did he usually talk like Senator Claghorne?"

"No, no. Only last night. It was something he said."

"And you don't know what it is now?"

Martha shook her head. "No, I don't. I wish I could remember because it was funny. I was feeling bad because he hadn't let me in and then I almost laughed when I heard it."

John thought this one over for some moments. When he looked again at Martha he obviously had an idea. "Was your brother ever married?"

"No, of course not. Never."

"He couldn't have been married secretly? I mean without your knowing it?"

"I knew everything about Merlin."

"I wouldn't be so sure about that, Mother," said Sandra.

"That's what I'm getting at," said John. "Could Mr. Broadstone have been married? Could he—pardon me for saying it so bluntly—but could he, whether he was married or not, have had a son?"

"I am sure he couldn't. Absolutely not," said Martha.

"It's a nice idea," said Sandra, "but it isn't the way

50

Uncle Merlin talked. I could almost imagine his having a child without our knowing it, but I can't ever imagine Uncle Merlin saying anything like 'It's a joke, son.' Uncle Merlin never told a joke."

"Oh, he *did*, Sandra." Martha sprang to the defense. "He always told a joke in his lecture. You know. That joke about the Swedish minister and the old maid. He *always* told that joke."

"Well, that's true," admitted Sandra, and she looked brightly up at John. "But he never told any other joke— not in his whole life."

"Speak up, son," said the Senator. "Don't just stand there. Speak up. Are they goin' to pin it on me or aren't they?"

There was nothing particularly son-like about Eugene August. Wiry, graying, perhaps in his middle forties—no one ever thought of Gene August as a son except those crime reporters who occasionally suggested that he was the direct descendant of Clarence Darrow. Certainly not since Darrow had the Middle West produced an abler counsel for the criminal defense. If, in the prisons of America today, there are frustrated electric chairs and underpaid executioners, no one is more to blame than August.

It had been something of a triumph for Merlin to persuade his galaxy of legislators and other notables to grace the opening of Broadstone. It would have seemed that his greatest coup had been persuading Gene August to spend a week on the island. The fact was that Merlin's invitation had arrived a few hours after Gene's physician had ordered him to indulge at once in rest, and in some exercise more healthful than twisting juries around his fingers.

Gene stood by the mantel in his room and on it rested the elbow that was already calloused from a hundred judge's benches. Trained to conceal himself behind an expressionless exterior, he was revealing none of the distaste he felt for Happy Ned Drumbow. Happy Ned, his thumbs looped into his vest, straddled a straight-backed chair with such an air of impatience as would have led one to believe that he was in the Senate chamber and a Republican was speaking.

"I don't see what you think they are going to pin on you at all," said Gene.

"The man welshed on me, didn't he?"

"Yes, so you tell me. He said he'd buy your island and then he didn't."

"And I was right put out with him, wasn't I?"

"True," said Gene.

"Well, down in my part of the country we might shoot a man for that."

"But you say you didn't shoot him."

"That's right," said Happy Ned. "That's what I say. But suppose the police don't believe me. I can't afford any scandal. I'm up for renomination this year."

"You mean re-election."

"Down where I come from we call it renomination. I'm tellin' you our state hasn't ever sent a man suspected of murder to the United States Senate." Drumbow's voice trailed off, almost with a hint of uncertainty.

"Just what is it you want me to do, Senator?"

"I want you to tell me how to handle it so I'm not

52

suspected. You're a criminal lawyer, aren't you? You ought to know your job. I know mine. If you come to me and tell me you want the cotton tariff fixed, I know what to do about that. That's my job. You ought to know yours."

"I still don't see it," said Gene. "Sure, the police may find out about your island deal and then they'll know that you were pretty sore at Merlin. But then what? Right away they'll want to know where you were this morning when the murder took place. By the way, where were you?"

"I was in my room. I just finished writin' a letter."

"When was that?"

"Before breakfast."

"How do you know that's when the murder was committed?"

"That's when everybody says. Everybody 'round the hotel says it was 'round quarter of seven."

"Right. You were writing a letter. That's some evidence anyway. Where's the letter?"

"I don't know."

"You mean you lost it?"

"I mean somebody stole it. Somebody rifled my room. I tell you they're out to get me."

"Was there anything incriminating in the letter?"

"As one married man to another, there was."

"Oh," said Gene, "the ground is getting more familiar. Just because somebody stole a secret love letter out of your room, though, is no reason to think that somebody is trying to tie you up to the murder."

"But suppose I told you that the letter was written to

a certain member of Merlin Broadstone's family? I'm not sayin' it was. But suppose I said it was." Happy Ned pushed nervously up from the chair.

"Did you say anything about Merlin in it?"

"Well, not directly. It was just a kind of—oh, you know"—Happy Ned brushed it off with a gesture—"one of those kind of romantic letters you write, and I was tryin' to make the lady know how sweet and pretty I thought she was, and so I was comparin' her kind of favorably to her uncle. I was tryin' to say somethin' about her bein' a rose growin' in a kind of cactus patch. You know. One of those letters." The room shook as Happy Ned paced around it. "I tell you I'd give two years of my seniority on the Public Lands Committee to know who stole that letter. What I was wonderin' was couldn't you maybe scout around and find out who stole it."

"I am not a private detective," said Gene, "and anyway I am down here for a rest."

"One thing's sure. It isn't in my room. 'Cause I looked." And Happy Ned, standing near the door, cast an eye all around Gene August's room as if to show just how he had looked. Then his gaze halted and in a few gangling strides he crossed to the opposite corner, bent down, and picked up something so small that Gene could not even see it.

"Pin," said Happy Ned. "You might have stepped on that. Those maids are careless." He dropped it in an ash tray on a table next to Gene.

Gene looked thoughtfully down into the tray. Only two feet from it, he could scarcely see the minute object that the worried legislator had spotted from twenty feet away.

54

FOUR

WHEN John and Sandra were last seen by us, they were standing in Merlin's room and it was approximately 11 A.M. Now it was two in the afternoon and nothing is known of John and Sandra during this interval. Certainly they had not been seen in the hotel. Certainly they had not eaten lunch with the rest of the people on the island. All that is known is that where they were, what they talked about and, indeed, what they were doing, subsequently proved to have had nothing whatsoever to do with the major events of the day. It was their own private business and, whatever its nature, it resulted in their approaching the hotel in the early afternoon, walking closely together and arm in arm. As John explained it to himself later, they had reached a point at which not much more could be done until he had interviewed Daniel Joyce. For Daniel was, obviously, privy to any number of facts which John now needed—facts about Merlin and his testamentary affairs. And Daniel had not been available for some hours. The medical examiner had taken one look at that twisted leg and ordered Daniel to the mainland, where there were X-rays, anesthetists, capable bone men, and plaster of

55

Paris. So, if a lieutenant of police had to wait until a leg was set and a patient returned from the mainland to the island, who but some cranky taxpayer would carp at his strolling on the beach or talking earnestly in a secluded corner or doing, indeed, God knows what with a girl who looked like Sandra?

Sandra pushed back a disarranged curl of her pageboy while John rapped politely on Daniel Joyce's door.

"Come in," said a voice. It was the voice of Arthur Hutch.

Daniel seemed to have taken over the bath chair on a permanent basis, but now he looked cared for; his leg, encased in spotless plaster, was lying on the upturned footrest of the chair. Arthur was, as usual, sitting in a vast easy chair. John and Sandra sat down on the bed. They looked as if they belonged there.

"Well, sir," said John to Daniel, "you'd think you'd been skiing."

"Young man," replied Daniel, "if that is intended as the light touch, let us have no more of it. I feel as if I had been knocked down by a murderer and broken my leg on a slippery auditorium floor. I also feel as if I had been punched under the eye. And, to top it all off, as if I had just been compelled to indulge in a half-hour business discussion about the winding up of an estate of which I am already heartily sick." And he glared at Arthur.

"He resents me," said Arthur. "He complains about having to discuss immediate and highly necessary business details merely because his leg is broken. You don't hear me complain." Arthur looked around for confirmation. Evidently nobody did hear him complain. "And yet here

I sit," he went on, "carrying on a business discussion despite the fact that I am racked by athlete's foot. I am telling you, Hugo, if your police force is worth a damn you'll track down this pedal poisoner. By the way, on this other little business—have you caught the murderer yet?"

John leaned back on his elbows. "Not quite. I am hopeful that Mr. Joyce will be able to help us."

"Do I look," said Daniel Joyce, pointing pityingly to his foot, "as if I were in any condition to go gallivanting around this island catching a murderer?"

"Oh, we'll catch him," said John. "You just tell us who he is. That attack on you in the auditorium lobby couldn't have been a coincidence."

"Thank you," said Daniel. "It didn't seem so to me at the time."

"What did happen in the lobby, Daniel?" asked Sandra. "Did you see the man?"

"*Was* it a man?" asked Arthur.

"Well, I'll admit it was dark in the lobby when I first went into it, and I didn't get a really good look at who it was. But it had to be a man. You don't think any woman could have done this to me, do you?"

Nobody argued the point with him, but in the silence each was considering the underdeveloped stature of Daniel Joyce and the various medicine-ball-tossing amazons about the island.

"Let's take it from the beginning," said John. "What happened?"

"Well, I had a bad night last night," began Daniel. "My sinus was bothering me quite a bit. During the evening Sandra and I had been up on the roof. I shouldn't

57

have gone there. It was really quite damp and chilly. I woke up this morning much too early. I guess I was the first person in the lobby. When I'm home, I have found sniffing some water and salt up my nose helps these sinus attacks. But just try to get some salt around here until the dining room opens. Then I remembered the Gulf and thought I would go down to the beach and scoop up some natural salt water."

"Was anyone in the lobby when you went out?" asked John.

"I suppose so. I think someone was behind the desk with his back turned. I didn't pay any attention to him and he may not have seen me. I went out the door nearest the elevators and walked around the hotel to the auditorium side. I was going to go on down to the beach when I heard this sound."

"What kind of a sound was it?"

"Well, it was really a sound stopping. I heard somebody walking in the auditorium and at first I thought it was one of the watchmen. And then, just as I was passing the doors, the sound stopped. Two of the doors were wide open and I thought it was funny that whoever it was didn't just keep on doing whatever he had been doing. I don't suppose I look exactly like the intrepid type, but I am curious. So I went up the steps and into the lobby. It was pretty dim in there. The sun had just barely risen. I thought I saw somebody over in a corner near one of the big pillars, and I called to whoever it was. I was pretty sure somebody said, 'Come here a minute.' I was hearing pretty well this morning because I had just put new batteries in my hearing aid. Well, like a damn fool I walked into the lobby and then it happened."

"What happened?"

"I'm not too clear about this because the thing knocked me out for a minute. But somebody jumped at me and socked me very hard and, when I went down, my leg slipped on the tile floor, and that's how I broke it. But I could swear that I saw whoever had attacked me go out through the door right afterwards just before I lost consciousness. And, more than that, I could swear that he was wearing a green jacket. You see, with the sun just rising it was quite light outside but still dark inside and I just had this flash of him when he hit the sunlight at the entrance."

"Can't you tell us more than that?" said John. "Was the person tall or short, fat or thin?"

"I'm afraid not. I have thought a lot about it since then. In the first place he was moving very fast, and in the second place I was pretty groggy from the blow."

"Well," said John, "would you say that it was somebody as heavy as Mr. Hutch?"

Daniel looked appraisingly at Arthur Hutch while Arthur looked much more appraisingly at John.

"Could be."

"Or, could it have been anyone as small as Mr. Hutch's son?"

"Say," said Arthur Hutch. "Aren't there any other standards of measurement around here?"

"Don't worry," said John. "I'm just using examples. For that matter could it have been a woman in slacks? Say somebody as slim and, er—well, somebody as slim as Sandra here?"

"It could have been somebody as something as anybody. I simply don't know. My primary impression was that it

59

was a man and my secondary impression was that I did not care for his type." Joyce paused, then went on. "The doctor on the mainland says I'm lucky my cheekbone wasn't smashed. He says I got a very powerful blow here." And gingerly he touched his fingers to the great purple welt below his eye.

John leaned closer to Sandra and whispered something into her ear. "No, of course not," she said. "Go right ahead. I don't care if Uncle Arthur knows about it now."

Arthur looked owlishly at her but said nothing as he drew a cigar from his coat pocket and seemed to concentrate on separating it from its cellophane.

"You were going to speak to Merlin Broadstone today, weren't you, Mr. Joyce?" said John.

"Yes, I was."

"Suppose you tell us your version of what that interview was going to be about."

"Sandra wanted me to make a deal with him. She wanted me to try to get a cash settlement now for herself and her mother. In exchange for which they would both have been willing to be cut out of the will."

"How do you think Mr. Broadstone would have reacted to that?"

"Not too well. I didn't tell this to Sandra, but I doubted if he would go for it. God knows he had plenty of money. But any sort of a settlement now would have meant giving up a certain part of his capital and I don't think he was prepared to do that until he died."

"Just how rich was he?" asked John.

Daniel and Arthur regarded each other cautiously.

"Oh, I know," said John. "There's no reason why you

60

should tell me. But on the other hand it's something the police could find out. What's the point in concealing it?"

Arthur shrugged, and Daniel mirrored it.

"After his estate is settled and assuming the sale of his magazine and this place and his other properties— conservatively, you wouldn't be far out if you called it eight million dollars. Check, Arthur?"

"Just about."

"Do you mind telling me how the estate was to be divided? What sort of a will did he leave?"

Joyce fussed with the cord of his hearing aid as if stalling for time. "It is somewhat irregular to say this now, but I'm going to have to open up that will pretty soon anyhow. I wouldn't hesitate to say that the estate was divided between his sister Hester and his sister Martha, two for one. That is, two-thirds to Hester and one-third to Martha, so that eventually Carl, Joanna, and Sandra would all have equal shares. There are the usual provisions for additional heirs should Hester or Martha have had more children, or for that matter, had Merlin, himself, produced any."

"Then Mr. Hutch here wasn't in the will."

"No, he is not a legatee. But in the sense that he is Hester's husband, and manages her funds, I don't imagine he'll feel neglected."

Arthur started to say something and then closed his mouth.

"Yes, Mr. Hutch?" said John.

"Nothing," said Arthur.

Sandra giggled. "It was going to be an impolite wise-crack, only he thought better of it. He was either going to say, 'In the sense that I am Hester's husband I do feel neglected,' or else, 'Anybody who is Hester's husband wishes he occasionally would be neglected.' "

"She writes all my dialogue for me," said Arthur.

"No one else was named in the will?"

"Not as a legatee," said Daniel. "Mr. Hutch and I are in it as executors, and I am in as the drafter of it and, by implication, as the man who will take it through probate. But no one outside of his immediate family is left any money."

"How will this affect the children who aren't directly in the will? What I mean, Mr. Hutch, is even though they are not named in the will, Carl and Joanna won't do badly, will they?"

"I shouldn't think so," said Arthur. "I have seldom heard of the children of well-to-do parents starving to death."

"That goes for me, too," said Sandra. "Mother will probably turn all the money over to me to manage for her. That's close to three million dollars, isn't it, Daniel?"

"Yes," said Daniel. "Before taxes."

"You see, John," said Sandra, "as I told you this morning, it's quite a motive."

"Yes, Sandy," said John. Evidently in the last few hours they had not only progressed into the first-name stage but also well past the point where it was necessary to protest such absurdities as suspicion of guilt.

John pushed himself up from the bed. "Well, thanks," he said. "Oh, there's one other thing. When was that will written?"

Daniel looked thoughtfully at the cast on his leg. "I think it was about four years ago."

62

"That's right," said Arthur.

"Was Mr. Broadstone a wealthy man then?"

"Yes, indeed, although nothing like as wealthy as now. I think he probably had two or three million dollars then. Of course since the craze swept the country everything's changed."

"I'd like to take a look at this place," said John. "Can you show me the way to the roof, Sandra?"

"Yes, of course," she said. She rose and joined him at the door, which he opened.

The gray-haired juvenile desk clerk faced them. He might have just come there or he might have been standing there for quite a while.

"I beg your pardon," he said, "I wanted to speak to Mr. Hutch. I was told he was up here."

"Come in, Archie," said Hutch and, waving a careless hand at him, added, "this is Mr. Archibald, the chief room clerk here."

"Some of the guests," said Mr. Archibald, "are asking why they can't go into the court now. Some of them want to use the swimming pool. I thought perhaps, because they're important people, you might want to do something about it."

"That's up to the lieutenant, here," said Hutch.

"Yes, I guess so," said John, "but I'd like to have a close look at that pool myself first. In fact, I'd like to get into it before anyone else does. How about telling them that the pool will be available in an hour?" He turned to Arthur. "Think I could pick up a pair of swimming trunks around here?"

"Sure," said Hutch. "Down in the locker room."

"Thanks. Like to go for a swim, Sandra? And help me look for—well, whatever the hell I ought to be looking for?"

"Oh, yes," said Sandra, as if plunging for unknown clues was the most romantic idea she had ever heard of.

Various time studies made by independent research organizations have fairly well proved that a man can strip and get into a pair of bathing trunks in anything from eight to eleven minutes less than it takes a girl to undress and wiggle into a few square inches of minimal beachwear. John Hugo, a man of the world, knew this. Thus, when he emerged at the side of the empty swimming pool, instead of gallantly waiting for Sandra's arrival he plunged in with the full knowledge that he could tear off a mile or two and still get his wind back before she showed up.

Subsequently, in his official report, John Hugo wrote, "I then entered the pool and swam several lengths in a preliminary examination." Actually, the plunging in of John Hugo was a spectacle that would have made most men struggle back into their bathrobes and fade toward the locker room. He hit the water in a low flat dive that should have caused an enormous splash but which somehow left only a gurgle where his feet disappeared. He came to the surface a good ten yards from the end of the pool and uncorked an easy eight-beat crawl in which his arms devoured yards while his relaxed feet drummed with the steadiness of a high-powered outboard motor. One of the resort editors who happened to be looking from his window at the moment remembered the days when he had covered

64

sports for the *Yale News* and estimated John's time at approximately 52.4 for the hundred.

Evidently this preliminary examination revealed nothing, for after half a dozen lengths John curved to the auditorium wall side of the pool and, treading water about halfway from either end, began a minute examination of the auditorium's bricks.

Several things at once became evident: (a) they were bricks, (b) they were held together by mortar, (c) there was no aperture in them sufficient for a lead pencil let alone for the barrel of a .38 pistol.

John, at the wall and precisely midway between the deep end and the shallow end of the pool, let himself sink till his toes touched the bottom. The pool was about six feet deep here. He stood there, picturing the room as he had seen it that morning, remembering the body with its upward-coursing bullet track, recalling the partly opened window and feeling, despite all evidence to the contrary, that the shot simply had to have come from here. From somewhere near the base of this blank wall opposite Merlin's room.

He scratched his head, pursed his lips, started to emit a flabbergasted whistle—and then realized that his nose and mouth were under water.

He came up for air, and it was as if someone had banged him on the head with an oar. For Sandra was standing there just fifteen yards away, on the other side of the pool.

Sandra in a bathing suit shouldn't have been allowed. There are those who maintain that a beautiful woman, simply and frankly revealing her body, far from being a

65

lascivious spectacle, is one to arouse artistic appreciation in man. If so, John was no artist. What was aroused in him was an instant desire to get as close to this incredible spectacle as he could. He pushed his feet hard against the wall. Unfortunately, there were no timers there that day, for a new international record for the fifteen-yard dash was set.

"How's the water?" asked Sandra.

"Water?" asked John as if she had opened the conversation by introducing a new element. "Oh, yes," he said. "Water. It's fine."

Sandra ran lightly to the deep end of the pool, somehow floated up onto the diving board, poised there for a moment, took three balletlike steps to the end, and went high into the air. A stout woman, observing this play from a window, said to her husband, "Oh, look, a swan dive." This was nonsense. A swan is a large, ungainly, long-necked bird, unattractively covered with a mess of feathers. In not one single respect did Sandra resemble a swan. She resembled, in the opinion of John, the most beautiful girl he had ever seen, executing the world's most perfect springboard evolution. A whole delightful lifetime suddenly opened up in John's mind—a lifetime spent with this wonderful girl in swimming pools. And then, on more mature thought, he realized that this kind of life was, after all, limited and that there were even happier and more spectacular realms in which to share her company. He pushed off from the other side of the pool and swam rapidly down, meeting her near the bottom. Shoulder to shoulder, flank to flank, and arms linked, they shot to the surface. As perfectly adjusted to each other's motions as

66

if they were waltzing, they somersaulted backwards and went under again, delicate thrusts of their feet driving them to the bottom.

It was hard to say which of them saw it first.

It was lying on the bottom, only a few inches out from the base of the brick auditorium wall, glinting in, and distorted by, the shifting light that filtered through the disturbed water. Together they turned toward it. John's hand closed on it and they pushed up to the surface. They treaded water and looked curiously at it as it lay in his palm. It was about an inch long, perhaps a quarter inch in diameter: a cylinder open at one end and closed at the other.

"It's part of a bullet, isn't it?" said Sandra.

John shook the water from his eyes and looked at the markings on the closed end. "Yes," he said. "It's an empty cartridge case from a .38."

"Then the gun was fired from down here," she said.

He nodded. "From near the surface. The cartridge case would have sunk after it was ejected." He paused thoughtfully. The bullet *had* to have been fired from the surface of this pool. Yet Carl, who had reported the gun flash, had not reported seeing anyone who might have fired the shot.

"Sandra," said John, "was Carl telling the truth this morning or was he trying to mislead us? If he had seen somebody here at the pool, do you think he would have said he hadn't?"

"Why should he have said he had seen a gun shot if he didn't want us to know he'd seen somebody at the pool?"

"But whom would he be protecting if he did want to lie?"

"This family sticks together, John," she said, and started to swim away. She could have been talking about Carl, or it could have been a comment about herself. It began to dawn on John that he might get pretty far with this girl—but not necessarily far enough to solve a murder. What the hell, he thought to himself, you can't have everything, and, with a purposeful stroke, swam after her.

FIVE

Islands have a great capacity for introversion. Take England on a day when a Princess of the Blood marries, or Manhattan Island when the Yankees and the Giants meet in world series combat. At such times islands bend upon themselves an enthusiastic concentration which leaves no thought for such trivia as wars, earthquakes, or elections occurring beyond the waters that surround them.

Broadstone was no noble, extraverted exception among islands. It could become preoccupied with the best of them. Its preoccupation, of course, took forms which varied with the interests of the preoccupants. There was the self-concentration of the immediate family, which might be quiet grief or gnawing worry over questionings to come. Among the employees of Broadstone, from its executive staff to the polishers of Indian clubs and dumbbells, there was a deep concern as to how much longer the payroll would keep rolling. The sincere Broadstonites moodily contemplated, if not their navels, at least their stomach muscles and wondered who would now lead them safely through a world beset by starchy foods, bad-posture-inducing jobs, and tempting cigarette and whiskey advertisements. Finally, there were the notables, the eternal seekers after publicity—providing it was good—who wondered how, in the face of a police order that no one should leave this island, they could somehow remain invisible amidst the scandal which enveloped it.

The folk of Broadstone could be pardoned for this overweening self-contemplation. They were the focal point of an interest which, while they were rising, breakfasting, and adjusting themselves to the first aspects of a major murder, had spread on radio bulletins and early afternoon edition headlines with such speed that already, although it was but the third of January, the murder of Merlin Broadstone promised to be the news story of the year.

Three racing boat loads of telegraphic equipment arrived simultaneously around the noon hour, and before two o'clock the Associated Press, the United Press, and the International News Service had established wire-heads in the north lounge of the hotel. Newsmen already on the island promptly found themselves relieved of this unaccustomed news story as front-page by-liners flew in to lend the color of their writing and their imagination to what, in the hands of lesser reporters, would have been a dull accumulation of facts. An NBC vice-president phoned Arthur Hutch to examine the possibilities of re-enacting that morning's breakfast, with Tex McCrary and Jinx Falkenberg interviewing the family and other guests. CBS, in a flurry of frustration, searched Florida for Red Barber, who was resting up after the Orange Bowl game. Mutual tried to get from John Hugo an estimate of how many days the case might run and planned, if it seemed that it might run long enough, to originate from the island a series of open-end shows for co-operative sponsoring across the country. That afternoon Elsa Maxwell ran a special column headed "What Price the American Waist-line Now?" and those who saw it in advance were already talking excitedly about a possible Pulitzer Prize.*

The messages of condolence swamped all telegraph facilities. Some people sent two messages. Senator J. Howard McGrath of Rhode Island, for instance, sent one to Arthur Hutch expressing the deep sympathy of the National Democratic Committee, and another to Happy Ned Drumbow suggesting that if there were no other way of his getting off the island he should start swimming that instant. In a similar vein the Hon. Homer Bentley of Illinois received private advice from Carroll Reece suggesting that Bentley do nothing to spoil the beautiful Republican picture for '48.

At five o'clock that afternoon, America's Own Folk Singer, the Rhymin' Ranch Hand, scooped all other folk singers with his coast-to-coast broadcast of the ballad he had been writing since morning. It was entitled "He Ain't Breathin' Deep No More." There were rumors that Corwin was readying a show for CBS, and although no one knew exactly how he would handle the story, it had already leaked out that there would be a remarkable central portion in which the various muscles of the body identified themselves and spoke to each other in challenging accents.

* *Readers who know that Miss Maxwell's column is usually prepared a day or so in advance of its appearance may think that she must have had prior knowledge of the murder in order to cover it the afternoon of the day it was committed. They should not be thus misled into suspecting her of the crime. Miss Maxwell was merely being an alert journalist and, I am happy to say, positively did not kill Merlin Broadstone. A. G.*

To quench pessimistic rumors, the traffic manager of Seaboard Airlines Railroad announced that there would be no curtailment of West Coast passenger service: "We carried throngs when there were only Clearwater and Sarasota and St. Petersburg, and we'll go on carrying throngs even if Broadstone closes up. No man is indispensable to Seaboard." A New England manufacturer of big-game ammunition wired a hopeful inquiry as to whether the mighty frame of Merlin Broadstone had been brought down by one of their special elephant-piercing bullets (We Drop Them in Their Tracks for You). The public-relations counsel for a large Middle Western meat-packing firm phoned a bland inquiry to the medical examiner: Was it possible that his lifelong vegetable diet had made Merlin Broadstone especially vulnerable to bullet wounds?

Movietone News instantly alerted the camera crew which it kept permanently on Florida's East Coast for the purpose of photographing bathing-suited high-school girls throwing grapefruit at each other. This crew crossed the peninsula and arrived too late to photograph Merlin's body, but instantly set about getting a variety of shots of Sandra—a type of subject with which it was long familiar. *Time* got a real break because, the third of January being a Saturday, Broadstone's death neatly coincided with the day Lucemen usually start Timediting. They turned out a brilliant cover story which splashed the nation's newsstands a few days later—with an Artzybasheff drawing of Merlin's massive head against an imaginative background of writhing biceps tattooed with dollar signs. *Life* photographers hit the island in midafternoon and began snapping the series of shots which subsequently made that memorable feature, "Life Goes to a Murder."

Nobody was at all surprised when, shortly before suppertime, the aircraft carrier *Midway*, accompanied by two light cruisers and several small units of the Caribbean Fleet, came up over the western horizon. In fact, it was something of a letdown when it turned out that these vessels were on routine maneuvers and that their timely arrival had nothing whatsoever to do with any orders from an ever-alert Secretary of Defense.

"I am beginning to envy," said John Hugo at supper that evening, "those fictional detectives who are compelled to solve murders in lonely castles or on barren swamplands. I have so many spots in front of my eyes from exploding flash bulbs that I wouldn't be able to see a fingerprint if one were pointed out to me."

John did not make this statement aloud, as he was not accustomed to speaking to himself (years before he *had* spoken to himself for a time, but, discovering that he was both an indifferent conversationalist and a poor listener, he had abandoned the habit). He was sitting at the family table, but the family wasn't there. At least not at the moment. It seemed to him that, in comparison with this Broadstone clan, he was a light eater. At least of smörgåsbord. One rapid circling of the buffet table, a picking up of herring here, of celery there, a generous laying on of anchovies, a serving of potato salad, another of various pickled vegetables, had sufficed him. But not the poor bereaved. They had already stowed away as much as they could carry on oversized plates. Now they were off for seconds. He thought, as he craned toward the milling crowd around the great buffet, that he could see Sandra, and possibly Arthur, too, stifling their grief in heaping double portions. Doubtless, somewhere in the mob, Hester and Martha, Carl and Joanna were similarly mournfully engaged.

John was not only sitting at the family table, he was also occupying Daniel Joyce's chair. One might have said that he was not occupying Merlin's chair out of deference to the deceased; or one might have remembered that Joyce's chair was next to Sandra's and sensibly abandoned further speculation.

This was the first time that John had met with the whole family on an occasion which was not primarily official. He had a vague feeling that some sort of sympathetic statement was required of him. On the other hand, this family did not seem to be looking for sympathy. True, there had been a hint of tears in Martha's eyes this morning; and, sometime during the day, he had surprised an almost doleful look on Hester's face. But there hadn't been even that awkward attempt at real grief which he would have expected a murderer to have been smart enough to show. Or was the murderer—even smarter—refusing to single himself out by such display?

Hester and Martha were the first to return to the table. The others, carefully balancing their overloaded plates, trailed behind.

John, popping gallantly out of his chair, decided to resort to conventional condolence in the hope that one of them would be surprised into an implicating reaction. "I must tell you how much I admire your fortitude. I think

74

it's wonderful the way you're carrying on in spite of your great loss."

"I found one stuffed with cheese," said Sandra, floating into her chair and, reaching across the table, dropping a white-cored olive onto her mother's plate.

"This herring salad," said Arthur, his mouth full of it, "invariably gives me indigestion. It is, however, worth it."

Carl said nothing. It is probable that he hadn't heard John's statement over the crunching sounds of his own celery eating. Joanna looked at him blankly over a forkful of mushrooms; Martha never raised her eyes from the tomato with which she toyed. John knew the truth. He had known it, of course, before. This family was not bereaved. This family had lost a leader, a tyrant, a daily provider of security. In exchange for this bitter deprivation it had been compelled to accept eight million dollars. Why not go on eating? Merlin's in heaven and all's right with the world.

And then Hester rose. She stood there, one hand crumpling her napkin; her eyes either misty or distantly focused. John watched her face, suddenly aware that this woman might not be nearly so stupid as he had thought. There was sensitivity in her expression, and where there's sense there's usually thought. She looked down, over the great bulwark of her bosom; looked down, not at any member of her family, but at John.

"I'm sorry," she said. "I feel rather worn out. There's—there's been so much today. Will you excuse me?"

She walked from the table, slowly out toward the lobby.

75

There was something in the great back, the weary progress, the head still high, which reminded John fleetingly of something he had once read, or of a picture he had once seen. Something about a Roman mother.

The others went on eating, and nothing much was said.

Subsequently, it seemed to John that there ought to be a law against murder attempts while a smörgåsbord dinner is being eaten. What with the milling about, the almost universal desire for second helpings and for thirds, who can say where anybody is at a moment when a gun goes off?

And it certainly sounded like a gun.

It was at least five minutes since Hester had departed. Carl had gone toward the buffet meanwhile. The others? Well, he couldn't say for sure where the others were.

The sound came from directly outside the dining room—which meant from the road. It was a loud and vigorous bang. John, throughout some years in the Police Department and a longish leave of absence most of which he had spent between Normandy and the West Wall, had become accustomed to gunshots to the point where he did not jump when he heard one. Certainly he was the only one in the dining room who didn't jump. Certainly, also, he was the first one in the dining room to hear the long hiss that followed the bang and to recognize it for air escaping from a tire. So fast were his reactions that he had already set the whole thing down in his mind as a trivial incident of a blowout when he heard the scream. He was still holding his napkin as he crossed the lobby and dashed out into the road.

The two victims were instantly evident. One was the

76

left rear tire of a parked station wagon, and it was stabbed to the death. The other was clearly a human being, although only its lower half was visible. The upper half was thrust into the station wagon's right-hand rear door.

Even as John neared this body, it stirred; it yelled—and he recognized it as a yell from the same voice he had heard before; it struggled up out of the wagon, and stood with one hand clasping its right buttock and the other a bottle of what gave every appearance of being Scotch whiskey. Now that it was wholly out of the vehicle, identification was easy. This was Carl.

"What happened?" said John.

"Somebody tried to stab me. Look!" And he pulled his hand away from his trouser to show a gaping tear. From the noises he had heard, John had no doubt that somewhere below that tear was, at the very least, a healthy scratch. Carl, with understandable horror, was pointing at the wagon's tire.

Embedded in it was a weapon—quite a weapon. The end that was thrust out, away from the tire, clearly identified it as a chisel. The end that was in the tire was that part of the chisel which is seldom seen, that pointed icepick-like part which is usually covered by a smooth, rounded handle.

"It came right at me," said Carl. "I was bending over the car and it came right at me. And then it went into the tire."

"Turn around," said John. "Bend over." It was easy to see from the tear in the trousers that Carl had been struck by the chisel end. It seemed likely that it had come at him with such somersaulting force as to catch him thus,

77

go ricocheting off, and land with its deadlier end between the treads of what looked like a comparatively new tire.

"Where did it come from?" said John.

"How the hell do I know?" said Carl. "I'm telling you I was bending over. I was in the wagon."

John looked in and understood why. Four other bottles of Scotch lay there, under the raised rear seat.

"Is this your car?"

"It's Dad's," said Carl. "It trucks things from the dock to the hotel."

"Is that his whiskey?"

"No. I got it on the mainland yesterday. I was keeping it here."

"Why weren't you inside eating?"

"I was. Only all that herring made me thirsty."

"Well, stow it now. Better get upstairs and take care of that scratch. Got any iodine?"

Carl pulled the seat down over the Scotch and slammed the wagon's door. He still held the bottle in his hand. "This is an antiseptic."

John followed him into the lobby and paused to tell one of his policemen that somebody in the vicinity was tossing unhandled chisels; to order the removal of the weapon from the tire and its study for fingerprints. He was explaining that it was futile to search for a possible chisel thrower when his voice trailed off. He was fascinated by a two-man procession coming from the dining room. First came a bellboy, behind him Congressman Bentley. The bellboy looked frightened; the Congressman, concerned. John had heard of precisely such a procession from breakfast this morning. He strode across and entered the elevator with them.

"What's happened?"

"It's that Mr. Joyce," said the Congressman. "He's been hurt or something."

"They just phoned down," said the bellboy. "There's a murderer in this hotel. That's what. A murderer."

John, who had suspected this ever since eight A.M., stepped with them out of the car and into the fourth-floor corridor. The elevator operator, abandoned in his cage, called plaintively, "Hey, you're leavin' me all alone in this car."

John was first at the door of Joyce's room. It stood open. All that met his initial glance was the largest pair of buttocks he had ever seen. What must have been yards of dress material encased them. For a mad moment he could think only of what Gutzon Borglum could have done with this. Slowly a woman, her back to him, rose, and he realized that he had been looking at the noble posterior of Hester Hutch. What she had been bending over and thus concealing was now clearly Daniel Joyce, his wheel chair, and his outthrust, cast-encased leg.

Hester stepped aside, laying her hand on her bosom— and leaving room for any number of additional ones. John bent over Joyce. The lawyer looked terrible. His left arm hung limply over the side of the wheel chair. His right hand clutched at the dressing gown above his heart. His mouth was partly open. His eyes were nearly shut.

"What happened?" said John, and it occurred to him as he said it that this was becoming his entire verbal approach to the case.

Evidently Joyce was not entirely unconscious, for his left hand stirred feebly and motioned, for no evident reason, at the wall to his left.

79

"He saw him again," said Hester.

"Saw whom?"

"The murderer. He saw the murderer."

John turned quickly to Bentley. "See if you can bring him around."

Bentley ministered to Joyce magnificently. No Congressman could have done more. He went to the table next to the wheel chair, poured water from a pitcher into a glass, held it to Joyce's lips, and had the good fortune to have Joyce drink a little. He sprinkled a few drops on Joyce's face. The color seeped back; the mouth became firmer; the eyes opened enough to disclose pupils distended with fright. Bentley felt for Joyce's pulse and—his luck holding —found it.

"He's all right, I think," Bentley said. "Just shock."

John, intrepid as ever, repeated, "What happened?"

Joyce rolled his head a bit from side to side. "I was talking to Hester on the phone." He half lifted the instrument lying in his lap. Bentley took it and put it back on the table. "And right in the middle of the conversation, while I was talking to Hester, somebody broke some glass in the room next door. And then—it seemed just an instant later—I saw him out in the corridor, going past my room." Joyce started to shake, and for an instant it looked as if he would pass out again.

"Take it easy, Mr. Joyce," said John. "Who did you see?"

"That same man—the one who knocked me down in the auditorium—the man in the green coat."

"Did you see him better this time?"

"No. Just like before. Just a glimpse going by the door."

80

"Where did you hear this glass break?"

"In there," said Joyce, pointing to his left. "In the next room."

"Hold everything," said John, and he rushed out through the open door and went a few feet down the hall. Sure enough, the door of the adjoining room stood open. John entered. There wasn't much to see: only three things, really. First, the room was empty. Second, there was a sizable hole in one of the windowpanes, and, looking through this, John could easily imagine how a chisel might have gone through here and landed at the exact spot where it had met, if not its own end, Carl's. The third thing for him to see was not so obvious. It was a rather long scratch on the side of the door jamb, about four feet from the floor—such a scratch as might have been made by the chisel end of a chisel if someone were holding it by its point and raising it over his head to throw it.

John came back into Joyce's room. "You heard glass break all right," he said, "Somebody threw something through the window. Whose room is that?"

"That's Joanna's," said Hester. "You don't think they were trying to hit my child?"

"Well, not exactly," said John. "Tell me," he continued, "isn't your room right next to Joanna's?"

"Yes," Hester said.

"Then why," said John turning to Joyce, "were you having a telephone conversation with somebody only two doors away?"

"Hester wasn't feeling well," said Joyce. "She was nearly overcome at dinner and came up to her room."

"How do you know that?" asked John swiftly.

81

Hester broke in. "When I came up I passed Daniel's door and I stopped in for a moment to see if he was all right. Then I went on to my own room."

"Why did you phone her?" John asked of Joyce.

"I wanted her to read something to me."

Hester broke in quickly. "It was a paper. It was one of Arthur's papers about Merlin's business."

Joyce said, "It was part of a radio contract. I suddenly realized that we had some sort of a clause in it covering the event of Merlin's being unable to go on the show, and I wanted to know what it was. So I called her up, told her where to find it in Arthur's desk, and asked her to read the clause to me."

"So you were reading the clause when the glass broke?"

"That's right," said Hester.

"Then why didn't you hear the glass break?"

"But I did hear it."

"You didn't say so."

"You didn't ask me. I was reading the clause and there was this awful smash of glass. I was upset and I said to Daniel over the phone, 'What was that? What happened?' And when he didn't answer I thought something had happened to him and I came running down the hall and here he was"—she spread her hands expressively—"well, you saw him when you came in."

John looked at Joyce and then at Hester. Skepticism was all over him. He walked over to the wall between Joyce's room and Joanna's and tapped its surface with his knuckles. It was thick and solid.

"Now look," said John. "You two have gotten your stories together very pretty. But there's some things that

82

you can't put over on a policeman. You see, I happen to have studied the laws of physics."

"What are you talking about?" said Joyce.

"Your window is shut now. Has anybody closed it?"

"No," said Joyce.

"Very well then. A chi— a piece of metal going through glass twenty feet away from you couldn't possibly be heard from here. The sound couldn't possibly penetrate a wall as thick as this one. The sound waves would simply bounce back off your wall. Now one of you come clean— because both of you are lying."

There was a shocked silence. It lasted perhaps five seconds. It was ended by the tinkle of glass from the next room. It wasn't a loud tinkle of glass, but they all heard it.

John said, "Pardon me," and the expression might have been meant to cover his second departure from the room or, what was more likely, the horrid accusation he had just flung at them. He went out into the corridor and entered Joanna's room again. A young woman was kneeling near the window. She was dressed in the terra-cotta uniform of a Broadstone maid. With a dustpan in one hand and a small brush in the other she was sweeping the glass from the floor.

"Who are you?" said John.

"Who are you?" said the maid. "This isn't your room."

"I'm the lieutenant of police in charge here. I'm on this murder case."

The girl stood up. She was quite attractive. "I'm the maid," she said. "I'm on this floor."

"Why are you sweeping up this glass?"

"The housekeeper doesn't like us to leave it around."

"How did you know this window was broken?"

"I looked in the room. I'm on night duty and I'm supposed to look in all the rooms and turn down the beds. Is there a law against sweeping up glass?"

"There is when it's evidence."

"This?" said the girl, looking at the splinters in her dustpan. "Evidence?"

"It just happens," said John, "that only a few minutes ago a dangerous weapon went through this window and hit a young man who was looking for something in the back of a station wagon down there."

The girl sucked in her under-lip and bit it. Clearly she knew who among all the people on this island would have been looking for something in the back of a station wagon.

"Was he hurt?"

"No," said John. "Not much. Just a scratch."

"I—I got to go now," said the girl, and she rushed past him out of the room.

It wasn't much of a mystery to solve. But it was the best John had done so far.

John followed the girl to the door. "Just a minute," he called. She stopped at the corridor and looked back impatiently over her shoulder. "Did you see a man out here? Have you seen anyone in this corridor in the last few minutes?"

"No," said the girl. "I haven't seen anyone."

John came back into Joyce's room. He was surprised to see Bentley still there—forgetting that he hadn't dismissed him. The Congressman was standing near the window looking out of it. As John entered, Joyce and Hester finished a whispered consultation.

84

"Thank you, Congressman," said John. "We won't need you any more. Why don't you go down and finish your dinner?"

"That's all right," said Bentley. "Don't care much for that Swedish stuff anyway. That's mostly Minnesota and Michigan, you know. I'm from Illinois."

When the Congressman had left, John sat on the bed. "Mrs. Hutch," he said, "when you were talking on the phone to Mr. Joyce, was your door open or closed?"

"It was closed," said Hester. "I was going to take off my dress and try to relax."

"Did you take off your dress?"

"I didn't have a chance. Daniel's phone call came."

"Now that phone call—" said John to Joyce. "You just wanted to know about a clause in the radio contract?"

"That's right," said the lawyer.

"Why didn't you ask Mrs. Hutch to bring the contract to you?"

"Because when she left here she said she was feeling upset and she was going to lie down. I assumed that she had partly undressed and that it would be easier for her to read it to me than to put on a robe or something and come up the hall."

"But she just said she didn't have time to undress. So you must have known there wasn't time to undress."

The lawyer seemed confused and looked apologetically at Hester. "Well, I guess I must have thought it was more time than it really was. I mean—"

"Oh, Daniel," said Hester, "stop trying to protect me. It was about three or four minutes from the time I left his room before he phoned. He's telling you the truth."

85

"Well, then, are *you*, Mrs. Hutch?"

"Well, yes," she said. "I mean I went into my room and —well, I guess I did have time to undress only I must have stood there looking out of the window a few minutes —longer than I thought."

"What did you see out of the window?"

"Nothing. Just the island. Water."

"You didn't see the station wagon on the road?"

"No, I wasn't looking down. I was looking straight out."

"Just looking out the window?"

"Yes," said Hester, "and crying a little bit, too." And she returned John's gaze unblinkingly.

SIX

BEFORE Merlin had hacked away its center and erected the quadrangular pile of Broadstone, the island's most notable feature—and the one which had recommended it most often to passing boaters—was its beaches. An unbroken periphery of fine, white, yielding sand allowed itself to be tenderly nibbled at by the Gulf of Mexico. A fringe of cedars looked down on this love play from a discreet distance of about thirty yards above high-water mark. Within this ring of cedars stood the palm groves, and, immediately inside these, the single motor road ran from the dock at the far end of the island, circled once around the hotel and splayed into various service drives. A stroller on the beach, particularly in the evening, had a sense of security.

No one, except perhaps some prying puritan on the roof of the hotel, could possibly have seen anyone standing on the particular stretch of beach once known as Tuna Tessie's and recently renamed by Merlin "West Cove." Merlin had been deeply shocked to learn of Tuna Tessie and of how this one stretch of particularly secluded beach had come to bear her name. Tuna Tessie, for more than fifteen years, had been the only woman to operate a fishing boat in these waters. Of all the fishing boats thereabouts, hers had been the smallest. Whereas most of the others set out with parties of from four to eight, Tessie somehow never seemed to fish with more than one sportsman at a time. It was also claimed that any fisherman who failed to make a strike by noon never caught a tuna at all. For, at lunchtime, Tessie invariably steered ashore to this inviting bit of sand to cook lunch for herself and her companion, to recline lazily afterwards on the sun-drenched strand, and, it was rumored, to indulge in those refinements of sport which the hirers of more prosaic male fishing guides missed. Tessie had died a few years before Merlin bought the island. She had died of what the doctors called over-exertion—and this was very strange because, when the mainland natives came to think about it, she had in her career pulled in far fewer fish than any of her competing boatmen.

Neither Happy Ned Drumbow nor Joanna knew of Tessie's legend as they strolled in West Cove that evening. Joanna, enjoying the aforementioned security, enjoyed as well a tingling anticipation. She knew a little of Drumbow's reputation for filibustering and felt that no man with his capacity for sustained expression would be content to limit debate to the brief passage of the night before.

However, Joanna was not the first girl in history to mistake a great talker for a great doer. To her considerable disappointment, only her ear was being bent this evening.

"We're in trouble," said Happy Ned. Actually he meant that *he* was in trouble; but he was using a familiar parliamentary device by which an individual legislator, subject to some personal attack from outside the legislative halls, subtly suggests that not he alone but "we"—the whole legislature and therefore the whole people—have been attacked.

They had stopped on a little dune not twenty feet from the receding tide and Joanna, looking up at him, saw also the moon above his shoulder—its bland three-quarter face outdoing his in brightness and nearly matching it in expression.

"You should have had a letter from me," said Happy Ned. "I wrote it last night after I left you." And he turned from her and gazed manfully out at the Gulf. "It was a love letter," he added. "A mighty purty love letter."

"Oh, Ned," breathed Joanna. "Let me see it."

"I only wish to God I could." And there was a fervency in his voice greater than any Joanna had heard before. "It's gone. It's stolen. And"—here he lowered his voice dramatically as if revealing a new letter-writing technique —"it started out with your name and it ended up with mine."

"Stolen?" said Joanna. "Somebody stole your letter?"

"*Our* letter," said Drumbow. "It's worse than cattle rustling."

"You don't think Mother could have gotten it?" It was Joanna's concept of the worst thing that could happen to any erring maid of thirty-two.

"Your mother!" said Drumbow. "Does she vote Republican?"

Joanna considered this question—not its implications,

the question itself. "We were never able to find out, Ned. In the last election we all asked her and she said that for the life of her she couldn't remember."

"No," said Ned, brushing all this aside. "Your mother didn't steal it. I know damn well who stole it. It was stolen by the man who passed down my hall this morning before breakfast and saw me sitting and writing it, the man who left the dining room before I did after breakfast, the man who more than anyone else in this here hotel would want to get hold of a letter involving a decent married Democrat and another woman, the man who . . ." Happy Ned was at his best in a "man who" speech. He could have gone on forever—and many were the delegates to his state's conventions who would have sworn that in the past he had.

Had any such delegate been present, he could have learned a lot from Joanna. He could have learned how to stop this flow and how to cut short perhaps two hours of oratory.

"Who?" said Joanna.

Drumbow paused and let the two fingers that were pointing at the heavens slowly drop to his side. "Bentley," he said. "Homer J. Bentley, Republican, Illinois."

"Why did he steal your letter?"

"My dear girl," said Happy Ned—and in his tone was the impatience of an adult with a stupid child—"I'm a Democrat, ain't I?"

"Are you?" said Joanna. "I didn't know."

"My God," said Drumbow. "What did you think I would be?"

"It never occurred to me to wonder."

90

"I'm in the Senate, ain't I? I'm from the South, ain't I? You think I'd be a Republican or a Communist or something?"

"Well," said Joanna, "you're not the only Democrat in the Senate, are you?"

"No," said Drumbow, but there was an uncertainty in his tone which would have made a more intelligent hearer feel that there were times in these early days of 1948 when he almost thought so.

"Look," he said. "I'm coming up for renomination this year. There's going to be an election this year, you know."

"No, I didn't," said Joanna. "But that's nice. The last election there was such a good-looking man who rang our doorbell. I signed something for him."

Happy Ned was not interested in Joanna's political career.

"There's nothing the Republicans would like better than to smear me. They've never had anything on me. Now they got somethin'. Don't you understand?" he said. "A man in the Senate ain't supposed to go around with women."

"Oh," said Joanna. She was not convinced. True, she had never seen the Senate. Nor, for that matter, a monastery. Nevertheless she was sure they were a couple of different institutions.

Drumbow rushed on. "Bentley will send that letter straight to the Republican National Committee. And they'll spread it around. There'll be newspaper gossip about me—and on the radio too. The only break I got is Winchell's a Democrat. He'd never use it."

"What did the letter say?" asked Joanna.

91

"Ah, just things about you." Happy Ned dug the toe of his shoe into the sand. "You know the kind of thing. About how nice last night was and how pretty you are. That kind of stuff."

Joanna was touched. It was at such a moment that she would have wanted to be held closely. But instead Happy Ned merely put his hands on her shoulders and even shook them a little.

"We got to get that letter back," he said. "Chances are he's got it right in his room now and is plannin' to take it with him when he leaves. It's up to you. You got to get into his room."

"But how will I know when he's not there?"

"That's no good," said Ned. "When he's not there he keeps the door locked. I tried. Somebody has to get into that room while he *is* there. That's why it's up to you. You don't think a man who's tryin' to get me out of the whole damn Capitol buildin' is goin' to let me into his bedroom. But he'll let *you* in."

"Why should he?" asked Joanna.

"Why did I—why did I go walkin' with you last night? You play your cards right and he'll ask you up to his room." Ned searched his memory for a proper term. "You've got to *vamp* him," he said.

"But if he has the letter," said Joanna, "he knows I've vamped you already. He won't pay any attention to me."

"That's where you're wrong," said Happy Ned. "All the more reason. He'd like to get you away from me just the way he wanted to get his district away from Kelley."

"Who's Kelley?"

"Child," said Happy Ned, "don't you know anything

about democracy? Look. You got to do this. If you don't get that letter back, we're ruined. Our names will be a scandal. Now it isn't goin' to be too hard. After supper I saw Bentley comin' downstairs. Remember? He went upstairs with that bellboy and that police officer. Ten to one he's somewhere around the hotel now. You could go in there just as easy and get him to talk to you. And in no time at all you'll have him eatin' out of your hand."

"I don't know," said Joanna. "I don't know whether I can at all."

"Well, damn it all," said Happy Ned, "you did it last night to me, didn't you? You think a Republican is any harder to make than a Democrat?" And Happy Ned's voice trailed off, for he realized that he had stated here the question of his times and that before the year was out it would be answered by nearly fifty million Americans.

At a place like Broadstone, dedicated to health and peopled by devotees of muscle and circulation, one might reasonably have looked among the largest and most powerful to find the healthiest. None the less, it is possible that nobody at Broadstone was of healthier mind and body than Nancy Loomis. The starched terra-cotta uniform that she wore all day concealed the simple vigor of her body. But even without that uniform—as we already saw last night when Carl was in her room—there was nothing notably statuesque about Nancy. No, her health did not reside merely in the fact that she was neatly put together; not merely in a wholesome linking of joints; not merely in a hearty quilting of firm flesh. It resided in something healthier than this: something healthy that

93

was of the mind. Nancy Loomis had never had a nasty idea in her life—primarily because, to her, nothing was nasty. Consequently she did everything, and did it with a gusto that was not merely wholesome but actually tonic. Nancy didn't drink very much, but when she felt like a drink she took one. There were times when it was a joy to her to drag tobacco smoke deep into her not inconsiderable lungs, and, at such times, she smoked. Nancy enjoyed the company and, indeed, the proximity of men; she permitted no puritan strictures to interfere with her enjoyment. She might have been married half a dozen times—and, by the lights of some prurient folks, should have been twice that often—but she had never seen any particular reason for getting married. Until now.

On the night of January 2nd Nancy had been a sleepy young lady casually enjoying the company of Carl Hutch, who was gradually approaching that state of inebriation at which she could forget about him. By noon the next day—such is the grapevine that circulates backstairs in a great hotel—she was a wide-awake young lady happily determined to allow Carl's pursuit of her to develop into a successful capture—a capture which would see her borne off, conquered, into matrimony and with nothing less to show for it than an eventual one-third share in an eight-million-dollar estate. What could be more hygienic?

Nancy had grown up in Florida. As a pre-adolescent she had discovered the boredom of picking oranges and packing them. In puberty she had decided that high school need not be prerequisite to a movie career. At nineteen it seemed perfectly practical to take a job at Broadstone as

94

a maid: the tips alone should make train fare to Hollywood possible before the spring was over.

When you have awakened in the morning from a healthy sleep and discovered that, despite its dreamless quality, it has suddenly become immensely practical to make a certain young man the young man of your dreams; when that young man has taken his place in your romantic fancy because of his sudden precipitation in the direction of fortune; when that precipitation is a direct result of a murder, then it is perfectly natural for you to take more than a passing interest in the crime itself. When, moreover, your daily duty involves the cleaning of rooms occupied by the victim and by the most immediate of the victim's family and associates, nothing could be more natural than that, on the evening after the murder, you should have in your possession a considerable collection of trash.

In her few days' service as a maid, trash to Nancy had been exactly that: something found in wastebaskets and dumped into dustbins. But since early morning, when she had gone on duty after the first news of the murder, trash had taken on a new character. Here before her, as she sat on her bed in her tiny room, was the result of a careful culling of the fourth floor's wastebaskets. Here, at the very least, were items which might partly satisfy her natural curiosity about the case. Here, at the very most, were items which might deeply affect the young tennis player who had suddenly leaped over a golden net into her heart.

The young tennis player sat opposite her as he had the night before. Obviously, there being two glasses, one next to her and one next to him, he had just served. And furthermore, judging by the quantity of liquor in each, he had been guilty of a double fault.

"This one," she said—and she held up a fragment of white hotel stationery—"was in the Senator's room. That Drumbow fellow. He's sweet on your sister. Huh?"

"Could be." Carl shrugged his uninterest in his sister's love life.

"Could be? *Must* be. He calls her his desert flower."

"Let's see," said Carl, and reached across for it. There were only a couple of lines on the paper. "Hell," he said. "It's just the start of a letter."

"I know. Looks like he began to write it and then gave up. Maybe it was a bad try and he wrote it over. Anyway, you can see it's the beginning of a love letter."

"It's torn right across," said Carl. "Like he decided this one wasn't any good. I bet you're right. I bet he did start over."

She took the letter back from him. "Isn't he married?"

Carl said, "I think so."

"You'd never know it," she said, "from the way this begins." She tossed it back on the bed. "Now this one." She picked up a white envelope on which someone had scribbled. "It's all figures. See? He's added these things up." And she read aloud, "Assembled lots, $43,000. Riparian rights, $23,000. Existing structures, $19,000. Option on ferry, $1500. He's got it all totaled here. $86,500. What do you think that would mean?"

Carl didn't know. "Where did you find it?"

"In the wastebasket in that lawyer's room. The one right next to where I saw the man throw the knife this afternoon."

96

Carl sat up suddenly. "You saw the man who threw the knife?"

"Well, not exactly. I got there right afterwards. A second sooner and I would have seen him."

"But that's the one who hit me."

"I know," said Nancy. "You showed me all about it. It's really not much of a scratch."

"Well," said Carl, "it could have been. It's not his fault he didn't kill me."

"There's another figure down here," Nancy said. "It says 'Present market value $20,000'—and he's got a question mark after it. And then down under that he's got '$66,500' and he's underlined it twice, like he was mad. Do you think it could mean anything?"

"Well, sure it means something," said Carl. "Lawyers are always handling business deals. Only how the hell would I know what it means? Anyway, what's the difference?"

"You don't seem very interested in this," she complained. "There's a letter here that your Aunt Martha got, and here's a laundry list. 'T-shirts, slips, step-ins.' Say. I'll bet this is your cousin Sandra's laundry list."

"How can you tell?"

"There aren't any brassières on it."

Carl pushed himself out of the chair, twice covered the length of the room.

"What's the matter with you?" asked Nancy.

"Look," said Carl, "you're treating this as if it were a game. There's been a murder here and I'm worried."

"Why should you be worried?"

"Well, I've gained a lot by it, haven't I?"

Nancy opened her eyes wide. "You have?" she asked as if the thought had never occurred to her before.

"You know darned well I have. I told you about it this afternoon."

"Well, supposing?"

"Supposing!" said Carl. "Supposing they ask me to prove I didn't do it."

"You didn't."

"I know I didn't. But how can I prove it? You know where I was this morning? I mean early?"

"Sure. You were in your room. You told me you saw the gun go off."

"Yeah. But I can't prove it. And suppose they ask me where I was before that. Even five minutes before that, or an hour before that. Do you know where I was then?" he repeated.

"Weren't you in your room after you left here?"

"No. I'm telling you I'm in a jam, Nancy. I wasn't in my room or anywhere I can prove I was. What time do you think I left here last night?"

Nancy shrugged. "Around five, wasn't it?"

"Just about."

"Didn't you go right to your room?"

"I started to. But I was pretty tight."

"I know."

"I was just a little too tight to get there. I passed out on the service stairs. I just sat down on them and I guess I slept there for more than an hour. I woke up when I heard a door slam somewhere below me. I guess it was the carpenters coming to work. And then I went back to my room.

98

Just before I saw the flash. But I can't prove I'd been on the stairs. Nancy, would you give me an alibi?"

"How do you mean?"

"I mean if I've got to tell them where I was, would you let me say I was here all night until nearly half past six?"

She pushed the papers away from her and stood up. "I should say not."

"Oh, what the hell, Nancy! This is 1948. You're not disgraced just because you had a man in your room. It probably happens in Florida every night."

"I can't do it," said Nancy. She paused as if searching in her memory for something. "Did you ever hear of a moral turpitude clause?"

"Of course not. What's that?"

"It's what they put in movie contracts. What chance would I have to get in the pictures if I were the kind of girl that had men in her room?"

"Are you kidding?"

"Well, you don't understand. Lots of them do it, of course, but they're not supposed to and nobody can ever prove that they do. I've got my career to think of."

"Nancy, you've got me to think of. If you really loved me like you said this afternoon, you'd be more worried about what happened to me than about your career."

Nancy sat down again and leaned back on the bed, her elbows behind her. She wasn't looking at Carl but at the opposite wall. She did have her career to think of. Her two careers. Three thousand miles away was a possible career in Hollywood if she could get there and if, getting there, she were lucky enough to catch the eye of some producer.

99

But here, literally within arm's reach, was a more certain career—the career of being wife to one-third of an eight-million-dollar estate. A Klieg light's gold can be switched off.

"Carl, did you mean what you said this afternoon? Did you mean you really wanted to marry me?"

"Well, sure. You know that."

"All right, Carl. I'll tell them if I have to."

"That's swell, Nancy." He came over to her and rumpled her hair in his hands. "That's swell. Maybe you won't have to. Maybe they won't even ask. But it's nice to know you'll stick up for a fellow."

"Sure," said Nancy. She pushed her head back against his hands and looked up at him. "I guess love's like that."

Throughout this long day we have seen John Hugo devote himself to the detection of crime. We saw him talk at length and earnestly to Sandra in the morning in an effort to get some line on what happened when the body was discovered. We saw him accompany Sandra to the questioning of Joyce and Arthur Hutch. We saw him go swimming with Sandra in a dogged attempt to find the source of the fatal bullet. We saw him dine with Sandra in a further effort to learn more about this deeply involved family.

Now, in all justice, John was entitled to a little relaxation, and so he and Sandra were standing on the beach across the island from West Cove. Merlin, a regular poet, had named it East Cove.

It was amazing to see the change in this police officer who had spent the day talking of motive and opportunity, of automatic pistols, blank walls and hurtling chisels, it

100

was amazing—at least it might amaze someone—to hear him now talk of hair that glistened in the moonlight and of hands so small that two of them could be cupped in a fellow's palm. But John was like that, versatile.

It would have been difficult for an observer, had there been one, to say whether this was the first time John and Sandra had ever kissed. And the very difficulty of this deduction suggested rather clearly that they were more than casually attracted to each other. When two people kiss for the first time, there is about the act a certain intensity, deriving chiefly from curiosity and discovery, which, when they are less than totally in love, subsequent embraces lack. But closeness and contact do not dissipate the fervor of true love. Rather, each succeeding contact increases the desire for further ones. Thus John clung to Sandra and Sandra to John with a passion which could have been either the at-last-released tension of a couple which had been meaning to do this for quite a while but hadn't yet got around to it, or the increasing heat of two who had been at it for a little while and were delightedly discovering that it was better every time. The problem which faces us, however, is not when John first kissed Sandra but rather: Who killed Merlin Broadstone? Seekers after the other fact are doomed to disappointment.

First kiss or tenth kiss, it was undoubtedly a profoundly meant and well-executed performance. Moonlight, which was otherwise quite visible on the stretches of East Cove, was undetectable between their clinging bodies. From a distance of a few feet away it would have been hard to say at precisely what point ran the more or less vertical line between them. It was a line which here merged and there

101

disappeared in mutually exerted pressure. Here was a white linen suit. There was a full-flowing green wool skirt and a long-sleeved embroidered blouse. Here clearly was a man's ear. And there, by deduction, a woman's ear beneath a pageboy bob. Here, because it was on our side of them, was a man's nose. There, presumably, but totally invisible, was a woman's. Had one wanted to photograph this scene—and what admirer of the good and the beautiful would have not?—the dim light would have called for an exposure of perhaps as much as two or two and a half minutes. This would have been entirely possible. A psychologist, observing them, would have said that here were two people emotionally enmeshed with each other, mightily attracted by each other's components of physique and character, impelled toward each other by powerful inner drives and deep need for expression. An urchin seeing the same scene would have understood none of these things and in his dumb childish way would merely have taken a stick and scrawled in the East Cove sand, "John loves Sandra."

They had just reached the cove. Now, they sighingly released each other and settled themselves on the beach. John on her left, Sandra leaned back, her palms placed behind her, her elbows straight. She knew that John was going to touch her and she wanted to be touched. But she was a little startled that his gambit should be quite so abrupt. Her elbow perhaps, her wrist, her waist—but this sudden pressure on the base of her spine seemed out of character with one who had been a gentleman all day. Still, it was John, and nothing John could do could be wrong. Shyly, she glanced across at him and then jumped a little.

102

For John's hands were folded across his stomach.

Who then, or what then, was at the base of her spine? She inched forward and put a startled hand behind her.

"What's the matter?" said John.

"There's something," she said, and then her hand closed on it. There was indeed something. It was large; it was cold; and, as she lifted it up, it was heavy. She swung it around in front of her and held it in her lap.

"It's a gun," she said.

John had come forward on his knees and was bending over the object.

"You're damn right," he said. Instantly he had a handkerchief out of his pocket and now the gun was cradled in its folds.

"Is that—is that it?" she asked.

"It could be. It's a .38." He lit a match and held it steady for a few moments. "Somebody filed away the serial number. That means it wasn't a pro."

"Why not? If it's filed away, you can't see it."

"We can't. But there are ways. Those numbers are stamped deeper in the metal than any file can reach."

Sandra looked behind her; through the palm trees the face of the auditorium was barely visible in the moonlight.

"So he comes out of there—the man with the green coat —and he throws the gun here. It makes sense."

"It does," said John. And he stood up.

"What are you going to do?"

"I'm sending this back to the mainland right away. I want them to check and make sure this is the same gun that killed your uncle. And then they can search it for fingerprints too."

103

"After it's been in all this sand?"

"Could be. Although I'm pretty sure we're not going to find any. Damn!" he said. "I did want to talk to you. I did want to talk to you for just a little without this murder breaking in. Come on," he said. "Let me turn this gun over and then maybe we can have a minute to ourselves."

It was a pity. Here the murder was nearly thirteen hours old and John and she had known each other for almost half a day. And still they hadn't gotten much further than most normal couples do in six months or so.

SEVEN

THE events of the next half hour were considerably confused. They were the sort of events which, in any proper
story of detection, would be set down by the detective in
the form of a timetable. However, it has long before this
become obvious that there is no detective in this story
capable of creating such a timetable. Hence we are going
to have to do it for ourselves.

When we last saw Carl and Nancy Loomis, they were in
Nancy's room examining the trash from the fourth-floor
wastebaskets. Almost immediately thereafter Nancy had
glanced at the alarm clock on her bureau, noted with
dismay that it was several minutes past nine-thirty, at
which hour she was due on the fourth floor of the hotel to
turn down beds and perform other nightly duties. Carl, as
Nancy rushed from the room, acted with what might have
been sheer absent-mindedness and picked up Drumbow's
abortive letter and the laundry list, stuffed them inside the
envelope on the back of which Joyce had made his mysterious fiscal notes, and stuck the whole business into
the pocket of his dark-tweed-flecked-with-blue-and-yellow
jacket.

It was nine fifty-five when Joanna, arriving from West Cove, came into the lobby of the hotel bent on Bentley and stopped flatfooted—a rather natural pose with her—when she found the Gentleman from Illinois standing not more than thirty feet away engaged in what might have been casual conversation with Carl. Her problem, obviously, was to get rid of Carl before she could begin the vamping of the Congressman. Carl, who was facing her, saw her enter, said something quickly to the Congressman, crossed to her, and urged her by her elbow out of the hotel. There was nobody else on the concrete walk where they stood.

"I want to talk to you," said Carl; which was indeed news, because this brother and sister seldom bothered with each other. "You'd better watch yourself."

"I'm really quite busy," said Joanna. "Can't we talk about whatever this is some other time?"

Carl held her firmly by the elbow, emphasizing his desire to do the talking then and there. "Do you know that Drumbow character is a married man?"

"Really?" said Joanna. "Most men his age are, aren't they?"

"Well, they shouldn't be when they're playing around with unmarried women. You watch yourself or you'll be in a jam."

"I can take care of myself," said Joanna, not bothering to deny the implied charge. Instead she said, "Just what do you think you've got on us?"

"He's writing you love letters," said Carl. "If they get into the wrong hands they could do you a lot of harm."

Joanna thought that over. It seemed clear enough. Drumbow had told her he had written a love letter. Drum-

106

bow had said that Bentley had stolen it from him. Bentley had just been talking to Carl. Now Carl was telling her about such a letter. Bentley obviously was a first-class rat.

"Look, Carl," said Joanna, "I appreciate your telling me, but I knew about it already. I'm going to get that letter away from Bentley. I know it's up in his room, and he had no right telling you about it."

"The hell it's up in his room," said Carl. "I have it right here." And he drew the envelope from his pocket.

That was nine fifty-eight and a half, and on this instant, as Carl held one half of the envelope, and Joanna the other, an unmistakable heavy footfall came around the corner of the hotel, and Arthur Hutch appeared.

Among all children who happen to be related to each other as brothers or sisters there is an unwritten and usually unspoken conspiracy against their parents. Next to having his father find out about his own derelictions, the last thing Carl wanted was to have his father find out about his sister's. Carl and Joanna exchanged a swift, understanding glance. Carl's hand fell away from the envelope. Joanna's hand thrust it into the pocket of her skirt.

Arthur regarded the two of them sourly. "This is refreshing," he said. "Have you two really given up sex or am I to infer from this that you've taken up incest? We are, you know, still supposed to be running a hotel." This last was addressed directly to Carl.

"What's the matter now?" said Carl.

"If you can remember," said Arthur, "the laughable fiction under which it was arranged for you to spend the season here, you were supposed to be responsible for stewardship. I'll admit that there are no bar stewards here

107

to keep you really interested, but you may recall your agreement to help the housekeeper check up on the maid service."

Carl nodded wordlessly. He remembered this very well and, in a sense, felt that he had performed his duties admirably.

"There have been two complaints," said Arthur, "from the fourth floor tonight. A lamp burned out in room 412. And whoever is in 428 has been trying to get a softer pillow all day. I think you'd better get up there and see that the maid on duty on that floor takes care of it."

"Right-oh," said Carl and dove into the hotel with genuine alacrity.

"As for you," Arthur said to Joanna, "God knows you're of age, but there is an impression around here that you are spending an inordinate amount of time with Democrats."

"I'm merely trying to be pleasant to the guests."

"A little more bipartisanship would seem to be indicated." And then Arthur hesitated, for out from the hotel came Bentley of Illinois.

"Good evening," he rumbled politely to Arthur. And he paused as if he had no intention of strolling on alone.

Joanna nodded sweetly to Arthur. "Yes, Father," she said, and placed polite fingertips on Bentley's crooked arm. Arthur shrugged and turned toward the hotel. It had been a long time since he had gotten such immediate obedience from both his children.

"Nice evening," said Bentley to Joanna, and started walking with her away from the hotel.

"You—," said Joanna, and indulged in quiet invective unlike anything Bentley had heard addressed to him since he had stopped ministering to patients. Somewhere in the midst of this invective, Bentley heard the term "stolen letter." Having recently stolen one, he singled this out for immediate denial.

"Why, what do you mean?" he said. "Who stole a letter from who?"

"You did," said Joanna. "From Senator Drumbow. And not only that but you tried to get me in trouble with my own brother."

"What?" said Bentley. And here he was on firmer ground, though no firmer grammar. "I showed no letter to no brother."

"Just what," said Joanna, "is your game?"

"I have no game. I wanted to talk to you. I've been watching you ever since I got here. I think you're a very attractive girl, and I wanted to talk to you like this, alone. Only I didn't think you'd be saying such terrible things to me."

"Why did you show the letter to my brother?"

"I didn't show the letter to anybody."

"Ah," said Joanna. "Then you admit that you stole the letter."

"Ah," said Bentley, who knew a tactical opening when he saw one. "Then you admit one was written to you."

"People are always writing me letters," said Joanna.

Bentley glanced coyly at her. "I don't doubt it. Look. Do we have to be angry about this? You admit Ned Drumbow wrote you the letter. I admit I have the letter. That's politics. I give you my word that when I use the letter I'll keep your name out of it. There's only your first name there, anyway. I'll see that you're protected." He cupped her arm a little above her elbow. "You see, I really like you."

"I'll bet you're married, too," said Joanna. "Just like Drumbow."

"Naturally," said Bentley. "Most members of Congress are. It's easier for them to get elected. It gives them a certain air of respectability. You're not going to mind if I play some politics with your friend Drumbow? He's really a very low character. Should have gotten him out of the Senate long ago."

"Suppose I did mind?" said Joanna. "Would you leave him alone if I told you it meant that much to me?"

"I doubt it," said Bentley. "It would only make me madder at him. I'd be jealous."

This was good—to have a man saying these things. And it was even better to know that you had him more completely in your power than he suspected.

"You're going to be terribly upset," said Joanna. "But you haven't got that letter."

"Don't be silly," said Bentley. "Of course I've got that letter. It's in my room this minute, and my room is locked."

"Well," said Joanna. "That's where you're wrong. I'm not telling you where that letter is. I'm just telling you it's not in your room. It's been taken out of there and it's in the best of possible hands."

Bentley stopped and looked at her in the moonlight. "Do you want to bet?" he said romantically. "Come up to my room now and I'll show it to you."

"Very well," said Joanna, and turned with him back to the hotel. She might even have been thinking that here was a change from etchings.

110

We have already seen Carl hasten into the hotel. It took him less than a minute to get to the fourth floor, to find Nancy, and to forget entirely about the light bulb in 412 and the softer pillow for 428.

"Listen," said Nancy. They were in a corridor which, for the moment, was deserted. "Do you have that stuff? You know, the stuff I took out of the trash baskets."

"Oh, that," said Carl. "Yeah. I know just where I can put my hands on it. But look here," he said. "I was just talking to Joanna. She knows Drumbow wrote that letter to her, but she thought it was in Bentley's room. She was some surprised to find out that I had it."

Nancy wrinkled her nose in momentary thought. "She's right. You don't have it. All we had was just the start of a letter. Don't you remember? We both said that he must have thrown it away and started all over again. But what would it be doing in Bentley's room?"

"Drumbow told her Bentley stole it. Bentley's supposed to have gone into Drumbow's room and taken it out of there."

"Then it's in Bentley's room."

"I don't get it," said Carl.

"Look," said Nancy. "Drumbow starts to write a letter to Joanna. He writes a couple of lines and throws it away. Then he starts all over again. We have the one he threw away. Now if Drumbow told Joanna that he hasn't got the letter he wrote her and Bentley stole it, he's probably telling the truth. Bentley could use it—politically."

"Then if Bentley has it," said Carl, "and uses it, that will get Joanna into a jam. She'll be right in the middle of a scandal."

"Where's Bentley now?" said Nancy.

"I just saw him leaving the lobby. He was going out of the hotel when I came in."

"In that case," said Nancy, "I think we'll go to Bentley's room and steal that letter back. After all, we don't want any scandal in our family. We've got to protect our sister, don't we?" she said.

It takes more than a few minutes to enter a room with a passkey, to go through several pieces of luggage with sufficient care to leave the contents undisturbed, to find at long last a letter beneath a pile of shirts, to close the luggage and leave the room.

That's why Nancy and Carl had barely emerged from Bentley's room when the elevator stopped at the fourth floor and Bentley and Joanna appeared in the corridor.

Carl and Nancy didn't want to seem to be together, so Nancy went bustling into one of the empty rooms as any proper maid had a right to, and Carl strolled down the corridor toward his sister. His sister paused as if she were going into *her* room. And Bentley, ignoring all three, walked purposefully toward his own. That left Carl and Joanna alone near the elevator.

"You're a darling," she said to him. "I can't thank you enough for stealing that letter."

"Well, that's all right," said Carl. "But how in God's name did you know?"

"What do you mean how do I know? You gave it to me," said Joanna.

"No," said Carl. "I didn't give it to you. But I've got it now and I'll make sure nobody gets it again."

112

"Carl, you mustn't drink so much," said Joanna. "It does things to your memory. Now I want you to go right to your room and lie down."

"I'm going to my room all right," said Carl, "but I'm just going to put that letter away."

"Dear boy," said Joanna soothingly. "Don't be too disturbed when you find you haven't got it. I have it now."

"You're crazy," said Carl.

"You're mad," said Joanna. And on this note they parted.

Bentley's door was open. Joanna stood in the doorway and looked with some amusement at the spectacle of a frustrated Congressman tearing frantically through folded shirts.

"I told you you don't have it any longer," she said.

"But it's impossible," said Bentley. "It was here less than half an hour ago. You know what?" And there were both conviction and righteous wrath on his face.

"What?" said Joanna.

"Somewhere in this hotel is a thief. A letter-stealing son-of-a-bitch."

"Well sure," said Joanna and looked at him sternly.

"No, no," said Bentley, "I mean *another* one."

Not even the best of detectives can drive relentlessly toward the solution of a crime without once pausing to look back upon the way he has gone. Few can work at all times alone. Thus, to John came the moment when he had to review his case, to reconstruct. So he had returned to East Cove to concentrate, and had, quite naturally, brought with him somebody to help his concentration.

"Darling," he concentrated.

"Yes, dear." Dr. Watson's voice was never so soft and warm as Sandra's.

"Merlin was shot at twenty of seven this morning. That is, if we believe Carl's story. The bullet was fired from outside his room. So it had to come in through the window. The direction it took in his body means it had to be fired from below, presumably from the swimming pool. And we have certain corroborating evidence."

His toe touched hers. She didn't pull her foot away.

"In the first place, there's Carl's story of the flash from the pool." He ticked it off on a finger. "Secondly, there's the fact that there's nowhere else on that wall for the shot to come from. Third, there's the cartridge case you found in the pool."

"*You* found it, dearest."

"No, it was you."

"*We* found it, then."

"Yes, *we* did." He smoothed her hair where it lay on his shoulder. "And then there are the pajamas. There was no hole in them." He struck a match, held it to two cigarettes, and gave her one of them. "Yet, he was wearing them when you found him. So somebody put them on him after he was shot."

"True."

"Why would anyone have put on his pajamas?"

"I can't imagine. Ever."

"Me either." He smoked for a moment more. "And how did anyone get in to put them on him? You said that door was locked."

"Absolutely." She pressed his hand.

114

"Of course," he said, "someone might have had a duplicate key—one that we don't know about. But, hell, that wouldn't make sense. Why go to all the trouble of shooting him at long range and from an impossible position when you've got a key to his room? Why not walk in, shoot him, and walk out again? And why, if you've got a key, use it for that nonsense with the pajamas?"

"Maybe there were two of them," she said. "Two murderers or a murderer and an accomplice. One shoots him from outside while the other puts the pajamas on him."

"Why? Why should any two people do that?"

"I don't know. But it had to be something like that. Didn't the medical examiner say that Merlin died instantly?"

"Yes, dear. What about it?"

"And Carl said that right after he saw the flash from the pool, those two brown things came out the window. Well, if Merlin died instantly he couldn't have thrown the slippers out afterwards. Somebody else must have done that. Wait a minute!" She smoked furiously. "Look. Suppose when the bullet hit him he jumped into the air and then as he fell to the floor, the slippers flew off and out the window."

"Uh-uh, sweet. When somebody gets hit by a .38 he doesn't jump into the air. He just drops in his tracks. But hard. Anyhow, even if your theory could be correct, why would he be wearing slippers but no pajamas? Those pajamas *had* to to be put on him after the bullet went into him. Why walk around stark naked, but wearing slippers— unless the floor was cold? Linoleum can be cold."

Sandra shook her head, and then brushed a lock of hair

115

out of his eye. "Not Uncle Merlin. He wouldn't admit a floor was too cold to walk on."

"Then why?"

"I don't know—unless he was afraid of athlete's foot, too."

"Was he?"

"The subject never came up. But Arthur had it, or at least he said he had it. Now, if Arthur had been walking around in Merlin's room barefoot, then Merlin would have been wearing slippers as a protection against the athlete's-foot germs that Arthur would have left there. How's that for a theory?"

"Terrible."

She took a pensive final drag on her cigarette and shoved the stub into the sand. "Do you think Carl could have been mistaken about the flash—or the time of it? He *was* hung over."

"Sure he could have been. But I see no reason to doubt his story."

"Why didn't anyone else see the flash, then?"

"I thought of that. It was the hour when everyone would have been showering or dressing. Those rules of Merlin's are some help to us. We know what everyone was supposed to be doing."

"Well, why didn't anyone hear the shot? At least, the ones who weren't under the shower—say! For that matter, why didn't Carl hear it?"

"Didn't he?"

"He didn't say so, John. He just said he saw the flash. And when he was trying to prove to us that he saw it, wouldn't he have said he'd heard the gun too if he had?"

116

"By God, you're right. And a gun fired in that courtyard would have made an awful racket."

"Unless it was fired under water."

"It couldn't have been."

"Or unless there was a silencer on it."

"Nope. I examined the barrel. Nothing had been clamped on it."

The silence was moody—or perhaps only sleepy.

"Gee. It's really tough. Do you think we'll ever figure it out?"

"Got to. It's my job."

"Maybe there's some angle you haven't even thought of yet."

"I'm sure there is. Only what it might be, and when I think of it, Lord knows."

"John. I've an idea. Look, this doesn't solve the business about the pool or the shot not being heard. But it could answer the pajama problem. Maybe he never had the pajamas off at all. Maybe he was taking them off, pulling them over his head when he was shot and then they fell back into place as he dropped to the floor."

"For heaven's sake, Sandra. Didn't you ever notice a man take off his—I'm sorry, of course not. Well, like most men's pajamas, Merlin's unbuttoned in front, they don't go over the head."

"Damn," she said. "I thought I had something there."

"Don't worry. It was a good try."

"But not good enough. Oh, John dear, I'm afraid I'll never make a detective."

He patted her soothingly. "Stop fretting. I could have sworn you had."

EIGHT

I<small>F GOD</small> had a sense of drama—or, for that matter, even a sense of fair warning—thunderheads would have rolled upon the island at dawn of the second day. But just as yesterday's deceptively placid dawn had failed to herald murder, today's was a dead-pan sunrise giving no hint of the chaos the morning would bring.

Arthur Hutch saw that dawn from the East Cove beach. He sat on a shapeless, dried-out hunk of driftwood, chewing an unlighted cigar and staring thoughtfully toward where the gray sky was turning pink. He watched the expanding areas of color critically, observing how the undersides of light cumulus clouds began to glow as the still-hidden sun touched them. He spat out a chewed-off sliver of tobacco.

"Rosy-fingered, my foot!" he muttered.

Arthur was in no mood for picture-postcard scenic effects. He was too aware of the several-million-dollar investment whose eight stories towered behind him, and of the uncertainty of its future. Would Broadstone now lend itself to profitable operation? Should he try to run it, himself, for the benefit of the estate? Should he throw it

118

on the market? And what of The Health Hour? Was there any way of continuing that program now that its principal figure had definitely and permanently gone off the air? What effect would the death of Merlin have on the sale of his books? How would the magazine fare, with Merlin off its masthead? These were troubling problems, and they had awakened Arthur at five A.M. Unable to sleep further, he had dressed and come to the beach in the hope that lapping waters and blushing skies might provide pleasant obbligato to quiet and constructive thought.

He struck a match savagely and drew impatiently at it through his cigar. Down the long barrel of the stogie, he glared at the visible semicircle of the Gulf of Mexico.

As if business problems weren't enough, he was at the focal point of various disturbing personal matters. His daughter was obviously involved with a cracker-barrel Senator. And something about the way she had sidled off last night with that horse-doctor Congressman had failed to reassure him. He firmly believed that girls should be girls, but he felt that Joanna, at thirty-two, should be a little more discreet about it. A wee touch of girlishness in her approach might make her seem less like a member of Canada's Royal Mounties. And then, there was his son. A sensible father, he was resigned to the fact that the boy would frequently leave his own bed unslept in. But why did he always have to look like hell the next morning? In *his* time, a young man appeared refreshed, reinvigorated —oh, well. Nor was he entirely comfortable about Carl's stellar role in the Merlin shooting. Why did he have to be the only witness? And such a nervous one at that? What had Carl and Joanna been so secretly discussing when he had come upon them the night before? And for that matter, he was rather puzzled by his wife and sister-in-law. Why were Hester and Martha taking their loss so stoically? And Sandra—she was behaving like a young gazelle set free. This last he could understand. John seemed a nice chap—although not too bright. They were a handsome couple. His thoughts dwelt enviously on them for some moments. And then those thoughts returned to business. He looked at his watch. Pretty soon he'd go up and talk to Daniel Joyce. He urgently needed to bounce his own economic thinking against the mind of the little lawyer. Of course, that might not be so smart: how much could he really trust Joyce? Indeed, whom could he trust?

These were moody thoughts. And so he rose moodily and walked slowly to the water's edge. He stood staring down at a lapping wavelet which ran up to within an inch or so of his heavy brogans. Still moodily, he flicked a cigar ash into the wave and watched with satisfaction as the tiny undertow carried the ash away. He sighed wistfully. He'd never been able to persuade Hester to furnish the house with really man-sized ash trays.

With a sad grunt Arthur turned his back on the sea. Which means that he turned his eyes toward the hotel. But he didn't see it. He couldn't see it. The man standing there about eight feet from Arthur, and on a slightly higher portion of the beach, totally concealed the hotel from Arthur's view. This was partly because the man bulked so large and stood so close to him that he filled Arthur's whole angle of vision. And partly because a small breeze was billowing the man's toga and this made him even more eye-filling. As he stood there with a suitcase in his hand, he seemed a quite young man and he was bending on Arthur a calm, indeed detached, gaze.

Arthur returned the gaze, but with less detachment, trying to decide how one opened a conversation with a man who, wearing a toga, has been standing behind you and observing you for God knew how many minutes. Finally the answer came to him.

"Good morning," said Arthur.

"Good morning," said the young man, carefully putting his suitcase on the sand. His voice was an uneven tenor, with timbrous baritone flecks in it. It seemed to Arthur exactly like a voice which only recently had stopped changing. It had also, obviously, stopped talking. Arthur felt the need of keeping the conversation going.

"You're new here, aren't you?"

"New?" The young man clasped his hands thoughtfully behind him and looked down momentarily at his Grecian sandals. "New? Why, yes. The wholesome body is ever new."

Mentally, Arthur staggered back and clutched his astonished forehead. Actually, he stood his ground and in a strange half-voice said, "Where—where did you hear that?"

"My mother read it to me when I was a child."

"Oh, I see." Arthur wiped sweat from his mental brow. "In a magazine, I guess, one of those health magazines. Or maybe a book."

The young man shook his head. "No, in a letter. A letter from Founder."

"Founder, eh. Let's see, that's a town, isn't it? Somewhere in the East, I believe. I'm sure I've driven through it. Who do you know in Founder?" Arthur felt a desperate need to establish some basis of sanity if not of the commonplace. He was terribly afraid of what the young man would say next. He said it.

"Founder is Founder. You must know him. This is a small island. What's your name?"

"Arthur Hutch." The reply was both meek and fearful. "What's yours?"

"Lovechild." The young man stepped forward, extending a hand which had to be hidden to be believed. "I'm pleased to know you, Uncle Arthur."

Actually shuddering, Arthur put his hand in the young man's; but the grip was gentle. "What," Arthur asked, "did you say your name was?"

"Lovechild. Lovechild Jones Broadstone."

"Jones?" quavered Arthur, almost hysterically. "Wherever did you get that name?"

"It was my mother's."

"She married—er, Founder, eh?"

The young man looked startled. "Oh, no."

"Well, wasn't Founder—?" Arthur was trying to handle this carefully. Even in the midst of his panicky confusion he was dimly remembering the need for admitting nothing that might later be prejudicial to his side of a probate contest. "Look. Tell me, what was your father's name?"

"Why, Merlin Broadstone, of course."

"And that's Founder?"

"Yes. Mother taught me to call him that."

"And Jones was your mother's name?"

122

"Yes, Uncle Arthur."

"But you just said she didn't marry Founder."

"She didn't."

"Oh."

Arthur, now that the young man was standing next to him, realized that his original estimate of his size had been a bit hyperbolic. The youngster probably wasn't more than six feet seven. He may not have weighed much more than two hundred and fifty. A size nineteen collar would clearly have fitted him, and his sandals couldn't have been more than 13 EEE. But there were mysteries other than his physique for Arthur to probe. He sat down on the driftwood where we originally found him this morning and, because it was a noble hunk of rotting timber, motioned the young man to join him. The invitation was accepted and the noble hunk creaked under their combined quarterton.

"Uncle Arthur," said Lovechild.

Arthur relit his cigar and took a few puffs. He was trying to orient himself to the situation of sitting on a piece of driftwood with a young man who was built like Paul Bunyan, clad like a cross between a Greek's glory and a Roman's grandeur, and given to calling him "Uncle."

"Yes?" he finally asked when the cigar was going well again.

"Do you think I look like Founder?"

Arthur examined the possible answers to this question and their conceivable effect on any potential legal action.

"Well, yes and no." Let them take *that* into court, he thought. And then he followed with an even better thought.

"Tell me, er, Lovechild. Have you seen Founder lately?"

"Oh, yes." Lovechild nodded amiably. "I saw him yesterday."

"You don't say," said Arthur. Then like a rapier stroke, "Was he wearing his pajamas?"

"No. He didn't have pajamas on. He didn't have anything on."

Arthur hid his excitement. "Where was he?"

"Stretched out there."

This was terrific. Arthur could feel his heart pound. "And what were you doing?"

"Watching the man comb his hair."

"What! What man?"

"The man in the undertaker place. Over there." And Lovechild waved a great arm toward the mainland.

"I see." Arthur relaxed in a mixture of relief and disappointment. "When was this?"

"Yesterday afternoon. Maybe near suppertime."

Arthur stared at his cigar for some moments. "Where do you live, Lovechild?"

"In New Jersey. Like always."

"With your mother?"

"No. Mother's dead."

"Oh, I'm sorry," lied Arthur. This seemed to remove one possible litigant, anyway. "Has she been dead long?"

"About five years. You see, they launched her once too often."

"You don't say," said Arthur.

"Yup."

They sat in silence for some moments.

"I beg your pardon," said Arthur, "but did you just

124

say something that sounded like your mother died because they launched her once too often?"

"Yup."

"Well," said Arthur, "just for a starter, who did?"

"Fellows who owned the cannon. There were two of them. They were named Angelo."

"Two cannons named Angelo?" stalled Arthur.

"Two fellows. The cannon didn't have any name. They used to shoot Mother out of it. Into a net."

"I see," said Arthur. "Carnivals, circuses, that sort of thing."

"Yes," said Lovechild. "I used to go to them with Mother when I was a kid. They were fun. Chasing the strong man and everything. She never went back to the pier, though. I wish she had. She used to tell me stories about the pier. That's where she met Founder, you know. The year before I was born."

Arthur cast his mind back over more than two decades. Yes, that was right. In the summer of 1927, at that big amusement pier in Atlantic City. Merlin had lectured there all of June. And there *had* been some sort of daredevil business with a cannon out on the pier's end.

"Did you see Founder often?"

"Not after I started to grow up. But he used to write. And he sent mother money every month. After she died he went on sending it to me. I was living with her father then on the farm."

That at least, thought Arthur, explained the rather large sums deposited regularly in a special account of Merlin's, and the checkbook he never let anyone else handle.

125

"Well, how did you happen to come down here?"

"Grandpa heard about what happened on the radio yesterday morning. And he came right in and woke me up and he said, 'Basty'—that's a nickname he always called me—'Basty, you better go right down there.' So I took an airplane."

Arthur regarded him in horror. "Dressed like that!"

Lovechild looked down at his antique costume. "Oh, no. I never had these things on before. I just put them on when the boat landed me here this morning."

"Why?"

"Mother always told me to be ready for this. She used to teach me Founder's exercises. And make me read his sayings. And she said if this ever happened to Founder I was to go ahead and take his place. She said, 'The faithful will follow you, Lovechild.' " The young giant stood up, smoothing his toga. "What time is it?"

Arthur glanced at his wrist watch. "About six-thirty."

"We'd better get going, then. I'll have to lead the morning Stretchings at seven. Will you tell the faithful I'm here and to be ready for me at seven?"

Arthur studied the massive form towering over him. "Why, certainly, Lovechild. Anything you say." Then he braced a little. After all, he remembered, this is merely my nephew. "As a matter of fact, down here Founder arranged for the faithful to take their first Stretchings alone in their rooms. Breakfast according to his schedule is at seven and the first mass exercise of the day is at ten. Now of course if you'd like to change that—"

"Indeed no. Whatever Founder ordered. Breakfast?"

"Yes. In half an hour. Suppose we go up to the hotel

and I'll arrange for a room for you. And, Lovechild, do you want to wear that—that costume? Founder always wore shorts."

"I know. I wouldn't dare try to imitate him. I'll just be modest and wear this. I only want to be myself."

"Of course. Well, let's get going; and—we'll use the service entrance, it's nearer. Also, do you mind breakfasting in your room? I'm afraid I won't be able to arrange a place for you in the dining room so quickly. And one other thing, after breakfast there's a man I want you to talk to, his name is Daniel Joyce and he's an old friend of Founder's. Do you know anything about law, Lovechild?"

"Not exactly. Except what you should and shouldn't eat, and staying out of drafts and reading in a good light— that kind of thing."

"Well, you'll *like* Mr. Joyce. Poor man, he broke a leg yesterday."

"I broke a leg once," said Lovechild, slinging his suitcase and striding up the beach with Arthur.

Arthur looked wonderingly at Lovechild's massive limbs.

"Oh, no," said Lovechild. "It wasn't one of my legs."

NINE

I<small>F IT</small> hadn't been for his still pain-racked features, his sedative-deadened eyes, the enormous cast around his leg, and the wheel chair in which he was imprisoned, you would never have known that Daniel Joyce had broken his leg the day before. He was nervously brushing crumbs of toast from his fingers and pushing his chair away from the table on which his breakfast tray lay, when Arthur Hutch puffed in. Joyce regarded him sourly. Indeed, his only gesture of welcome was the turning on of his hearing aid. But Arthur sat down on the bed not even looking at Joyce, much less speaking to him. Silently he began to take his own pulse. Some moments passed before this little tableau of invalidism was broken by Joyce's voice.

"Well?"

Arthur shook his head and moved his lips to indicate that he was intently counting to himself. Finally Arthur dropped his hand from his wrist.

"Fast," he said dolefully. "Seventy-eight. And no wonder. With how many new emergencies am I expected to cope?"

Joyce looked at him with the mild interest of a man

128

eighty per cent of whose attention is evidently focused on a fractured tibia.

"Who's dead now?" he asked.

"Oh, no," said Arthur. "Nothing as simple as that. Another death we could cope with. What we're up against is another life."

Joyce was startled into a momentary silence during which he tried to think which of the various women on the island could have produced this miracle overnight. Finally he gave up.

"I don't get it."

Hutch leaned forward. "Look here, Daniel. You and I are in a tight spot. We are the only two responsible people on this island. What's more, we are both far from well men. We can't have any secrets. We've got to come straight with each other."

Joyce blinked at him. "I thought I had been coming straight with you. Haven't you with me?"

Arthur Hutch ignored the question, topped it with one of his own. "Do you know anything about Merlin's private life that you don't think I know?"

"Good God, man, I was only his lawyer. You were his brother-in-law. You were much closer to him than I was."

Arthur shuddered at this memory.

Joyce went on, "What kind of thing do you think I know that you don't? What's up, Arthur?"

Arthur blurted, "Do you think it's conceivable that Merlin could have had a son?"

"Conceivable?" said Joyce. "A pretty choice of word. Merlin having a son, eh? Well, sure it's possible. I guess it's like a man writing a book. I read somewhere that everybody's supposed to have at least one in him. By the way," he went on, "if you just dropped in to ask that question and are thinking of leaving now, you might tell me first if Merlin did have a son."

"I don't know," said Arthur. "That's the whole question. You can't tell it by looking at a man."

Joyce put his fingertips together and appeared to be considering this from every angle.

"Well, for instance, if you saw a man holding a baby or walking a carriage . . ."

"Oh, hell," said Arthur, "that's the way you tell whether a man has a son. The problem here is whether a son has a father."

"Of course," said Daniel, "I don't know whom you're talking about. But as I understand it, no matter who it may be, the odds are enormously in favor of it. Listen, Arthur, are you or are you not trying to tell me that Merlin had a son?"

"God, no," said Arthur. "I'm trying *not* to tell you that. But the evidence is against me. This morning, only a little while ago, I'm sitting there and he comes up to me and he says, 'I'm Merlin's son.' Look," went on Arthur, "I'll give it to you from the beginning."

"I could use it like that."

With a fine feeling for physical detail Arthur told of his encounter with Lovechild. Joyce listened without apparent emotion, and of all the questions that he might have asked about the story at its end, he was content to select merely one.

"And how old did you say he is?"

130

"Twenty this year," said Arthur, "I told you that before."

"I know," said Joyce. "I just wanted to make sure."

Arthur got up from the bed and strode around the room, his head bent, his unlit cigar turning between his lips. He stopped finally in front of Joyce's chair and looked down at him.

"What does this do to us from a legal standpoint?" he asked. "I mean the will."

"That's easy," said Joyce. "You know the provisions in it for any heirs that might turn up. If you mean what does it do to us from the financial standpoint, well, if this character turns out to be what he says he is, it cuts Carl's and Joanna's and Sandra's eventual shares from thirty-three and a third per cent each down to twenty-five per cent each of the estate. Which still isn't bad." Joyce pulled at his underlip for a moment. "Of course," he continued, "it makes the probating of the will more complicated. At least it will drag out a little longer. Because if this Love-child is only twenty then under the law he is still an infant."

"Oh, brother!" said Arthur, "hold that thought, will you? He's right down the hall. I want you to see this infant." And he bustled out.

Joyce's expression didn't change. He continued to look rather blankly ahead of him and then absently took a roll of peppermints from his dressing gown pocket, put one on his tongue, and breathed across it thoughtfully. Fortunately, he was exhaling when Arthur re-entered ushering Lovechild ahead of him.

Lovechild stood quietly, well poised in the center of the

131

room while Joyce regarded him from head to foot. This was a process which even quick eyes could not have accomplished rapidly.

"Well, I'll be damned," said Joyce.

"That," said Arthur, "was precisely my reaction. Er, sit down," he said. And then the three of them looked about the room, searching for a piece of furniture sturdy enough for this purpose. Lovechild finally selected the bed. Its springs sighed under him and the other end of the mattress rose as if in an agonized attempt to escape.

"What's your name, young man?" asked Joyce.

"Lovechild Jones Broadstone."

"And who is your father?"

"My father was Merlin Broadstone."

"Suppose you had to prove that in court?"

"I'd look them in the eye."

Joyce rubbed his chin. "Well, just assuming they wanted a little more than that. Have you got anything— you know—evidence?"

The young man stood up and pulled open his toga in front. Both Joyce and Arthur started to recoil in horror— and recovered as they saw that he was wearing partly rolled up slacks beneath the Roman robe. Lovechild went into one of the side pockets and came out with a wallet. He unfolded this and slipped open an inner pocket and from it he extracted a twice-creased piece of black paper.

"Grandpa said I'd better bring this. It's a copy of my birth certificate." He handed the photostat to Arthur, who was nearest. Arthur examined it, grunted, and passed it to Joyce. Joyce looked at it cursorily and tossed it on the table beside him.

132

"This says that a baby named Lovechild was born to a woman named Jones and a man named Broadstone twenty years ago in New Jersey. But it doesn't say that you're the baby."

"Well, Grandpa would say so and there are two or three of Grandpa's old friends back home. They'd say so."

"Okay," said Joyce. "We'll skip that for a moment. Why have you come here?"

"For my inheritance, of course," said Lovechild.

"Just like that, eh? Pretty cold-blooded. And how much do you think it amounts to?"

"How much? Oh, you mean money!" Lovechild waved a protesting hand, and a slight breeze was felt some distance away. Then he dropped the hand and seemed to consider the point for the first time. "Money? Well, I suppose if there's money I would be perfectly glad to take care of any that I'd have to. I'm willing to do my duty. But that isn't what I came down for. I'm the only person who can succeed Founder, and I've come down to succeed him." He looked at the little traveling clock on Joyce's bureau and then at Arthur. "What time did you say we'd have the Stretchings?"

Arthur motioned him back to the bed. "Plenty of time. Just relax."

"It seems to me," said Joyce to Arthur in a tone he used to witnesses at moments when he was really addressing the jury, "that the whole question of whether this young man is or is not Merlin's son and rightful heir is secondary. The primary point is that if his story is true, he had a motive for Merlin's death."

The young man on the bed frowned; creases appeared

133

between his eyes; the corners of his mouth went down; his underlip pouted. On anyone else this juvenile grimace would have been laughable. On Lovechild it was rather awe-inspiring. Although the toga concealed every one of them, you knew that the young man's muscles had bulged. The atmosphere in the room altered. You could almost hear double basses throbbing out menace-music.

Arthur gave Joyce a nervous high-sign and Joyce hurriedly said, "Of course, I'm not accusing you."

The young man stayed his mood without relinquishing it—like a volcano trailing threatening smoke while waiting to see if the villagers at its base put enough sacrifices on the altar.

"You see," said Arthur, casually tapping the wrong end of his cigar into an ash tray, "we are all suspects—anybody who was around here when the murder was committed or anybody who stands to benefit by the death. You know how police are."

"I know nothing about police," said Lovechild and then, looking at the wall opposite him, went on as if reading words which had suddenly appeared on it. "There is no health without honesty. In the good man, conscience is the only law and sinews the only protection."

"Absolutely," said Joyce, forgetting in his nervousness to think of what place his profession would have in a society like that.

"We all agree with you," said Arthur, "but we've really got to introduce you to the policeman. I mean he's in charge here and police don't know all this about conscience. You don't mind if he comes up here and—you know—just asks you a few questions the way we did. And,

Lovechild, I hope you'll let me attend your Stretchings this morning."

This, evidently, in the eyes of both giver and recipient, was the ultimate sacrifice. The volcano stopped rumbling. The smoke wisped and disappeared. The sky was blue again. And that happy villager, Arthur, walked around to Joyce's phone and called the desk.

His inquiry as to John's whereabouts elicited the information that the indefatigable lieutenant was breakfasting with Sandra. Arthur told the bellboy to inform him at once that there was a new development in Joyce's room. He put down the phone and rejoined Daniel in silent contemplation of the new development.

When John Hugo entered the room with Sandra beside him he was a perfect picture of a tireless police officer who, although he may have been up all night working on a case, had needed but a hearty breakfast and a few cups of coffee to prepare him for whatever the day might bring.

And then, as he stood in the door, he saw Lovechild. Rather slowly he and Sandra crossed the threshold. And even more slowly John closed the door behind him. There was outright awe in their expressions. Evidently something about Lovechild struck a common chord in all men. For, after a moment, John said, "Well, I'll be damned."

"This," Arthur said to Lovechild, "is my niece Sandra Lockhart. Sandra, this young man wants you to know him as your illegitimate cousin Lovechild. Lovechild Jones Broadstone, this is Lieutenant John Hugo of the local police."

"How d'you do," said John, who knew a policeman's duty. "Where were you at six-forty yesterday morning?"

135

"In bed," said Lovechild.

"Yes, yes," said John. "But where? I mean what bed?"

"In mine," said Lovechild, "at home."

"Where's that?"

"Grandpa's. In New Jersey."

Daniel Joyce picked up the birth certificate from the table.

"Here," he said to John. "This may save you some time."

John came over to him and took the paper.

"This address where you were born. Is that where you were the night before last?"

"Yes," said Lovechild.

"How did you get down here?"

Lovechild repeated his story of a plane trip, of an overnight stay on the mainland, of an early morning arrival on the boat.

"You know, of course," said John, "that all this is easily checked up on."

Lovechild glared at the policeman. "Conscience and sinews," he seemed to be saying to himself. Aloud, he said, "I don't like—"

"Nevertheless," said John, "we'll check it." He stood his ground remarkably well. But then, only a few years before he had faced a German Mark VI tank which at the time had seemed almost as big as Lovechild did now. John bent down and said in Daniel Joyce's ear, "If his story is true, what's in the will for him?"

Daniel held up his right hand with two fingers showing. John nodded with lips pursed. Joyce lowered his two fingers and then raised his hand again as if to touch his

136

ear. "You know, Arthur," he said, "there's one thing about this that's not right."

"One thing!" said Arthur. "Nothing has been right since I got up this morning."

"We could be," went on Joyce, "in serious legal trouble. Here we are interviewing a claimant to the will and one of the ultimate heirs is present, but the other two aren't. True, you're their father. But I think, to put ourselves absolutely beyond reproach, we ought to have Carl and Joanna in on this too. I think they ought to have a chance to meet Lovechild as early as Sandra did and to question him if they want to."

Arthur shrugged. "It's all right by me." And going to the phone, he ordered his son and daughter paged and delivered to Joyce's room.

"Suppose—" John started to say. But Joyce stopped him short.

"Let's wait a couple of minutes. The other two will be here and then we can go on."

John stuck his hands in his pockets and leaned back against the wall.

Carl arrived first. It seemed he had been near by, acting out his stewardship by checking up on one of the maids. Carl's unspoken reaction to Lovechild was that of a tennis player who had finally seen somebody who couldn't possibly be passed at net.

Joanna, pulling in a few minutes later—she had been sunning herself in the courtyard—met her fate.

What are the components of love at first sight? For Tristan and Isolde it was a weak meshing of emotions which all too presently required the fortification of a love

137

potion. For Cinderella and the Prince it was briefness of
time combined with something of a shoe fetish. For Romeo
and Juliet it was parental defiance and their own attrac-
tiveness (of course they did wear masks on their first
meeting and stood in darkness on their second). For
Joanna it was simply that this was the biggest man she
had ever seen.

Examined even on the most superficial level, we know
that she had already dallied with Drumbow, whose most
outstanding physical characteristic was his height. A
little more profoundly, we might remember that both her
parents were outsize: her mother both bulky and high, her
father at least bulky. What more natural than her immediate attraction to the largest male she had ever en-
countered?

And what more natural for Lovechild than that he
should be immediately captivated by the first woman who
had ever been attracted to him? Love is reciprocal—
especially when all of your twenty years have been spent
on a rather lonely farm with a generally unattractive
grandfather.

As if in a daze—as if, for that matter, she had ever
been in anything else—Joanna came over to Lovechild.
Practically on tiptoes, this tall girl looked deeply into his
eyes—into those eyes which might have been borrowed
from a couple of Cyclopes. Something in them seemed to
fascinate her.

"They're Uncle Merlin's eyes," breathed Joanna.
"When he was young. That's how he held all those people.
That's where his power was. They're Merlin's eyes."

Lovechild did not know that this was the most profound

138

statement Joanna had ever made. He merely gazed back at her with reverence, sagging a little and leaning forward, his face like a huge and not entirely unhandsome pudding, and said, "I like your eyes, too." At first sight of his gangling but sympathetic and receptive cousin, Lovechild had come apart at the seams.

"Well now," said Joyce, "let's get on with it." And in a rather brilliant bit of summary he covered the events of the morning and brought the Hutch children up to date.

"So? Was he telling the truth?" asked Carl. And then Carl was treated to the rumbling volcano as Lovechild gathered his conscience and sinew. Perhaps Carl would have backed down right away, or perhaps it would have developed into something. They never found out. The Hon. Homer Bentley, Congressman from Illinois, prevented that discovery. He burst in. His face was red; his mustache ends were twitching like windshield wipers. He was breathing hard. Obviously there was something on his mind. Obviously, also, his powers of concentration were enormous. For, paying no attention whatsoever to a toga-clad, six-foot-seven-inch man in the middle of the room, he strode directly over to John and shook a finger at him.

"There's a criminal in this hotel and I demand that you arrest him."

"Now look here," said John. "We've known about that for twenty-four hours. We're doing the best we can to find out who he is."

"Ah," said Bentley. "You and your old murder! I'm talking about a crime that could shake this nation to its foundations. I'm talking about a crime that could rip

139

this government apart. Last night a letter was stolen from me."

"What letter?" asked John.

"Never mind what letter. Look, young man. I'm a Congressman. I make laws. You're merely a policeman. All you have to do is enforce them. I insist that you arrest the thief."

"Who?" asked John.

"That vote-buying—that—that *Democrat*, Drumbow."

"Did you see him steal it?"

"No. I didn't have to see him. I know he stole it. You just let me accuse him and watch his face."

"Right," said John. "I will." And he went toward the phone. But before he could touch it, it started to ring. He picked up the receiver.

"Yes," said John. "Oh, he did? You do? Well, come right up." He replaced the receiver. "That," he said, "was Senator Drumbow. He says you stole a letter from *him* and he wants me to arrest *you*."

Bentley waved this aside. "That's got nothing to do with the case. That was before. He stole it last."

Arthur cleared his throat. "Are you getting the impression, Lieutenant, that we are drifting an eentsie weentsie bit away from the murder?"

"I know," admitted John, "but what the hell am I to do? If a citizen comes to a policeman and says arrest somebody, a policeman has to look into it. Now listen"—and he swung back to Bentley—"I'm not going to give very long to this business. We're going to clear it up or throw it out." He went to the door, opened it, and stood impatiently looking down the hall. Presently they heard

140

the elevator clang and then the footsteps of a long-striding man.

Senator Drumbow's entrance was as precipitate as Congressman Bentley's had been. But he did notice Lovechild. In fact, he stopped and regarded him with what was at least interest and might have been envy. It was possible that some remote corner of his mind had been brushed by the thought that here, at long last, was a man who dressed as a Senator should. Then he spied Bentley behind Lovechild and pointed a bony finger at him.

"That's the thief," he said. "He stole my letter."

"Funny thing," said Arthur, sitting again on the bed. "He was just saying the same thing about you."

Drumbow, mouth open and about to reply, was conscious of a tug at his sleeve. He looked around to find Joanna behind him; a Joanna who had managed momentarily to detach her attention from Lovechild. "Pardon me a moment," he said, and turned his back on the rest of the room.

"Look," Joanna whispered, "It's all right. I've got the letter." And from her pocket she took the envelope that she had seized from Carl the night before—the envelope with the financial items scribbled on it, the envelope containing the laundry slip and the abortive letter. This letter she withdrew. Drumbow took one look at it and waved it aside.

"That ain't it," he said. "That's one I just started. It wasn't good enough." He turned away from her and, under his Neanderthalic brows, his eyes slowly swept the room. His left hand clutched his lapel, his right knee was flexed, his left foot advanced. As he opened his mouth,

141

everyone in that room shrank. The Senator was about to make a speech.

He began in a low register, hushed with sad incredulity. "He said I stole the letter? He impugned my honesty?" He bent his head under the weight of this injustice. Then bravely he flung it back and his eyes blazed. "Well, let me tell you that not in twenty-five years in local, state, and national politics has any man accused me of stealing and been able to prove it." Again his gaze swept them all. "I had a letter," he said. "The letter was in a desk. It was my desk. In my room." He paused to let them all absorb the unique circumstances which he had just revealed. "And"— his other hand went to his other lapel, and he bent forward—"it was my letter. I had written it." He turned, looking at them all, as if daring one of them to step forward and claim that he could not write. He went on, pointing a finger at Bentley. "He came into that room. He took that letter. Was it an open letter? It was not. It was a personal letter. Was his name on it? It was not—"

This fascinating examination of the letter continued for quite some time. Drumbow asked himself question after question, *and answered every one unhesitatingly and without a single error!* Under cover of this amazing display, Joanna sidled next to Carl.

"Wise guy!" she muttered. "You didn't get the letter. That wasn't it."

"I know it wasn't," whispered Carl. "That's what I was trying to tell you last night. But I did get it later, after I saw you downstairs. Forget it, it's in a safe place."

"Oh." It was genuine relief. Joanna relaxed and tossed the envelope on Joyce's table beside her. Its slip—the laundry slip, that is—was showing. Sandra, standing be-

142

hind Joyce, was four feet from the table, but she recognized it. A frown crossed her face. It might have been puzzlement. Joanna slipped back next to Lovechild and he bent on her a great bovine look of adoration.

"I stand here," went on Drumbow, who indeed still did, "a free citizen of the United States and a visitor to the Sovereign State of Florida. I came here in all innocence. I would, I now realize, have fared better if Mr. Broadstone had bought my island. Down my way the law is more rigidly enforced." He paused and looked at Joyce, who had some time before resumed his *Reader's Digest* in self-defense. "You too, sir, would have fared better. However, as a student of American history and of the many wonderful places within our great boundaries, I had never once been led to believe that if I were to come to the State of Florida and write a letter it would be stolen from me without my having the full protection of the State of Florida's laws. Mr. Joyce?" The little lawyer looked up from his little magazine. "You are a lawyer, sir," said Drumbow. "Is there not a law against letter-stealing in the State of Florida?"

Joyce pretended to ponder this. Then picking up the envelope that Joanna had dropped on the table, he popped it into his *Digest* as a bookmark—laundry slip and all. "Why of course there is," he said.

And behind him, Sandra, dropping a hand on his shoulder, almost imperceptibly patted it.

"Well then," said Drumbow, turning to John, "I demand the immediate arrest, trial, conviction, and incarceration of that low, slimy, Republican sneak thief," and he leveled a finger at Bentley, "the Honorable Gentleman from Illinois."

TEN

Not much more than an hour after the Senator's oration, Lovechild, on the great sun-drenched roof of the Broadstone, was leading the faithful in their Stretchings. That the men and women who for so long had bent and stretched, breathed in and breathed out for Merlin should now, without apparent wonder, be doing it for Lovechild; that their gyrations were being photographed by newsreel men, iconoscoped by television crews, and breathlessly described by radio announcers; that Lovechild was In, firmly entrenched and accepted, and that the word of his arrival was even now flashing across every news wire in the hemisphere—all this was the result of a few simple occurrences of the morning. In the first place, in spite of Arthur's effort to sneak Lovechild into the hotel, his presence there had not been kept secret. A waiter had served him breakfast in his room, and this waiter was just the sort of gossipy fellow who could not resist mentioning to fifty or sixty of his backstairs co-workers that room 420 was now occupied by a young man who stood six feet seven in his sandaled feet and who wore one of them Roman bedsheet things. Such word, via the servants, had spread

144

throughout the hotel. It had established what Lovechild looked like, but it had not revealed who he was. This latter information, about which the family might have been at least temporarily reticent, was spread by Drumbow and Bentley, the only outsiders who thus far had been privy to the secret of the young giant. They had talked about it —and talked about it where it would do them the most good. Both of them being men who needed the frequent friendship of the press, they had wasted no time, once they left Joyce's room, in passing this little tidbit out to every available journalist. Consequently, when Arthur attempted to lead Lovechild down the fourth-floor corridor and toward the roof for the exercises, they were met by a surging mass of reporters who demanded an interview, and on that instant.

Arthur protested, but quickly realized that the only possibility of ever getting Lovechild to the roof lay in first sating the curiosity of the press. So back to Lovechild's room they went and—with reporters perched on the furniture, squatting on the floor, leaning against the walls, and with a few luckless ones tiptoeing over each other's shoulders in the doorway—Lovechild held his first press conference.

Arthur tried to speed things up by giving a swift and reasonably accurate account of Lovechild's arrival on the island and of the relationship he claimed. This the press snapped up as a starving man would absorb a canapé and stayed on, with the same degree of hungry expectancy, to ask questions.

Did Lovechild remember his father? Could he remember his father way back when he, Lovechild, was a little boy?

145

Had his father loved his mother? Had his father's visits to his mother been frequent? Had they—er—tapered off in later years? Had (hopefully) his mother shown any sadness at this tapering off? Was his mother a nudist, too? His grandfather, perhaps? Did he mind wearing clothes himself? Where had he gone to school? What had he liked to study? Did the other boys play with him or was he too big? Did the girls play with him? Had he liked the girls? Had he liked any one girl more than any of the other girls? What had he done about it? If he were old enough, whom would he vote for this year? Who was his favorite movie actress? Had he ever seen a Tarzan picture? How would *he* like to live in a jungle and swing from trees? Had his mother ever taken him to Atlantic City? What had he done there? Had he ever seen the beauty contests? What had he thought of the last one? Did he think the current Miss America was pretty? If she weren't married already, would he want to marry her?

All this took about twenty minutes, at the end of which the press, not necessarily satisfied but laden with as much as it could transmit in one story, slithered off to phones and wire rooms. This left the photographers, who now had freer play for their flash bulbs and Speed Graphics.

None of this satisfied the newsreel, radio, or television men. But the announcement that Lovechild was about to lead his first exercises cheered them no end and they dashed to the roof to prepare their equipment.

At this point Arthur instructed the hotel staff to spread the word everywhere throughout the building and its grounds that special exercises would be held at once on the roof. He personally escorted Lovechild there and kept him

146

hidden away from the eagerly gathered crowd behind a couple of water tanks while he himself addressed the guests.

It was a simple, effective, and not unaffecting speech. Arthur realized that he was, in a sense, telling the bereaved about a reincarnation, that he was giving a peppermint stick to a child who had just lost a caramel, that his role was not entirely unlike that of the ancient heralds who cried, "The king is dead—long live the king!" He did not pretend that Lovechild would be their new leader. He merely told them who Lovechild was and said it was up to them to decide if they wished to be led.

When he finally produced Lovechild before them, there was a long sigh from the audience. It was neither the sob of the bereaved nor the joyous shout of the saved. It was much more the recognition of fulfillment. For years these people had so eaten, so exercised, so functioned that they might possess perfect bodies. Here at last was at least one. What more fitting than that their beloved Merlin, the preacher of perfection, should have produced a solid slab of it himself?

Either because he had a fine sense of the fitness of things or because it never occurred to him to do anything else, Lovechild's opening remarks bore the unmistakable touch of genius. He stood before them, looked commandingly around the entire crowd, placed his hands on his hips, and with majestic dignity said:

"Breathe in!"

They breathed in.

"Breathe out," he said and, although most of them would have done so anyhow, their breathing out was as a thing controlled solely by him. He extended his arms at right angles to his body. Every man and woman present mimicked. He swung his torso to the left. They, facing him, swung to the right. He twisted in the opposite direction. They turned with him. He bent forward and touched his toes. They became like a sea of waving wheat. He lifted his arms high above his head. They reached for the heaven which had been returned to them. He flung himself prone on the ground and pushed up once and twice and yet again. They flattened and rose and flattened again like undulant worshipers before their idol. He spun himself over on one hand and lay flat on his back. They likewise stretched themselves in the sun. He raised his legs in a great arc up over his hips, over his shoulders, over his head, and touched the floor behind him with the tips of his toes. Their legs rose, pointed skyward, and descended. He came back to his feet, stretched his arms again, flexed his knees. They followed every motion.

It was quite a show.

And quite a bit of work. The only one of the bunch who seemed to be breathing hard was John—breathing hard and seeming a little surprised at himself. He had been standing on the fringe of the crowd near the wall which encircled the roof when the exercises began. Perhaps it had been the magnetism of Lovechild or perhaps it was merely a vigorous young man's love for exercise; but, whatever it was, something had compelled John to go along with the gang. He had considered himself a pretty fair athlete, in pretty fair condition. Yet, he was astonished to find that this workout had made him puff a little whereas folks in his immediate vicinity who must have been twice his age seemed totally unaffected except for freshly glowing skins. Maybe, he thought for a moment, there was something in this calisthenics stuff after all.

There had been no reaction except a sigh when Lovechild had appeared and started. But now, as Arthur remounted the little platform, addressed the crowd, and told them that, although no permanent plans had been made, for the time being the hotel would remain open under its old management and the health of the guests would now be under the personal care of the new Leader, there was applause from everyone and here and there something like a cheer.

It remained to be seen whether Lovechild had it for the long run, but he certainly had looked good in the tryout. Arthur was quite pleased. He could scarcely wait to get over to the television boys to learn whether the new Leader was telegenic.

While his father introduced the new Leader to the faithful on the top of the hotel, Carl, clad in a pair of batik swimming trunks, sat in a deck chair beside the swimming pool and sipped at a tall glass filled with a brownish liquid which, by all the rules of Broadstone, should certainly have been prune juice. He heard the rhythmic slapping of sides as the exercises progressed above him. He heard the applause and the sporadic cheers which closed the ceremonies. Prune-juice fancier that he was, he went on sipping and staring absently into the hypnotic depths of the swimming pool.

Then he slowly put the glass down on the tile beneath the deck chair and with some surprise got to his feet, moved to the edge of the pool, and looked into the water. He went around the pool and out on the diving board, knelt at its end, and looked down again. Then, with the air of one whose curiosity has overcome his distaste, he dove into the water, swam rather awkwardly down one wall of the pool and along the bottom. Presently he came puffing to the surface, struggled quickly up the ladder, climbed out of the pool, stood dripping at its edge, and stared unbelievingly at a small object in the palm of his hand. He glanced up, looked rather frantically around the empty courtyard and, seeing nobody, shouted:

"Hey!"

The echo was fine, but that was all he got back. From the roof above him there was another outburst of applause. Whatever was happening up there, the Faithful were liking it. He looked again at the little object in his hand, then closed his fist on it purposefully, came around the pool, picked up a bilious-yellow robe from the deck chair, and strode across the court and into the lobby.

The sleepy policeman who had been sitting by the desk the day before was on duty there again. It would have been hard to say what this duty consisted of, but there is a tradition which calls for police to be stationed at such strategic points when a crime is being investigated.

Carl stood over him, waiting until the bluecoat's heavy lids lifted, and then opened his hand about ten inches from the bulbous nose.

The policeman looked, grunted, said, "Where'd you get it?"

"In the swimming pool," said Carl.

The policeman reached out a heavy hand and picked up the tiny thing in fingers almost too clumsy to handle it.

"Did you see the first one?" said Carl.

"Yeah," said the policeman.

"Like this one?"

The policeman shrugged. "Could be. Same caliber. In the pool, huh?" The policeman struggled out of his chair, went over to the desk, and picked up the phone. Evidently John had left word of his whereabouts, for in a moment the policeman put down the phone, resettled himself in the chair, and said to Carl, "They'll be down in a minute." Even in this brief time on the case, John was being referred to in the third person plural.

Carl leaned against the desk. The policeman turned the little gleaming thing over in his fingers. Time passed—not more, perhaps, than three or four minutes. An elevator banged open and John stepped into the lobby—alone.

With some distant bow to discipline the policeman struggled out of the chair again. He held his hand open as John came close to him. John, the policeman, and Carl stared down at the object. John picked it up.

"Where did you get it?"

"*He* got it," the policeman said.

"In the pool," said Carl.

John held the object closer to the light. "What part of the pool?"

"The far side. Near the blank wall. About midway along the bottom."

"How did you happen to see it?"

"I was sitting there looking at the water."

John turned it over in his head. "It's got the marks," he said. "Without a microscope you couldn't be sure, but I'd swear it's exactly the same." He reached into his pocket. There was a split second during which John looked

151

strangely puzzled; the policeman looked expectant; Carl looked blank. And then John was withdrawing his hand from his pocket again, and neither the policeman nor Carl ever found out what he had been about to say, because a bellboy came tearing into the lobby.

"Hey!" the bellboy yelled, "there's a fire!" and he went out through the door that led toward the west beach. They turned and over his shoulder as he went through the door they could see smoke: thick, oily clouds of it. It couldn't have been more than fifty yards away from the hotel. They ran and were on the bellboy's heels as he emerged into the sunlight.

It was a fire, all right. But it would never go down in the history of great conflagrations. In the midst of a little palmetto grove small orange flames danced over what couldn't have been described as even a bonfire. It was as if the contents of a wastebasket had been burned—no more than that. But it had been burned thoroughly and the oily color of the smoke was no mystery when they smelled the air. Naphtha or gasoline had been poured there.

The bellboy and the policeman and John stamped around on the embers. Carl, barefoot, wisely kept out of this exercise. Quite quickly, the fire was put out.

"I thought it was really something," said the bellboy. "I saw it from upstairs. It looked like a brush fire."

John was squatting, poking at the ashes with a stick. "It's cloth," he said, and he held up a piece a couple of inches square, half burned. The half that was not burned was clearly cloth; not only cloth but clearly wool; not only wool but clearly green. Carl, over John's shoulder, stared at it and snapped his fingers.

152

"Gee!" Carl said. "Yesterday morning when I found Daniel Joyce he said there was a man in—"

"I know," said John. "He told me."

"Is that it?" said Carl.

John turned it over in his hand. "Why not? It's green. It's wool."

"He must have had the wind up," said Carl. "He must have known you knew about him. But I swear I never saw anyone around here with a coat like that."

John shook his head. He wasn't listening. Or else he didn't want to. He had picked up another partly unburned piece. Along one edge of this there was a bit of smooth material, like a binding. John stared at the green fabric as a man would stare at something he once had known and now half recognized; and then he touched the binding with his fingers and closed his eyes as if remembering more by feel than by sight. He grunted and dove again into the embers. This time he picked up something too small for either of the others to see, something that he put in his hand and touched gingerly.

"What is it?" said Carl.

"It's an eye," said John.

"Cripes!" said the policeman, and drew back, horrified.

It *was* an eye: the sort of eye a hook goes into; a little bit of metal; a little bit of commonplace dressmaking metal.

"I never saw anything like that on a sports coat," said Carl. And then he paused and added, "Is there an Englishman here? They wear them. They got sports coats that fasten up under the neck when it rains. They got a hook and eye up under the collar."

153

John said, "Maybe. But there's somebody I ought to talk to." He turned back into the hotel and stopped at the far entrance. Sandra was there in the lobby with Joanna, and over them, above them, around them was Lovechild. He wasn't talking to them. He was merely looking at Joanna. He might have been a Saint Bernard and Joanna might have been a frozen mountaineer.

Sandra saw John and dodged out from between this enraptured pair.

"There you are," she said. "What happened to you?"

"Nothing happened to me," said John. "I was up on the roof exercising."

"I was there. I guess we got separated in the crowd."

John said, "There's been a little fire outside."

Sandra said, "Oh," and John said, "Somebody burned this," and held out a bit of the material—the piece with the binding on it.

Sandra looked at it and said, "The man in the green sports jacket." And John said, "Neat," and then added, "Ever see a sports coat with this on it?" He was pointing to the binding.

Sandra said, "I guess there are all kinds."

John looked at her and touching his finger almost tenderly to the binding, rubbing his finger along it, he shook his head. "You know the last time I touched this."

"I do?" she said. "I doubt it." And she turned back to Joanna and Lovechild.

The policeman re-entered the hotel and John whirled on him. "Get back there and collect every bit of those ashes. All of them. And if you find anything that looks like a zipper," said John, "bring it to me fast."

154

"Oh," said the policeman, "you think it was a whole suit, huh?"

"Never mind what I think," said John.

"Well, I only mean, Lieutenant," said the policeman, "some of them still have buttons."

"What I think this is part of doesn't have buttons," said John. He went back to Sandra.

"Look," he said to her, "I want to talk to you—alone if you don't mind."

Sandra shrugged and moved away with him.

"I know what this is," said John.

"Are you sure?" said Sandra.

"I know what it is but I don't know why you did it."

"Maybe I didn't do anything," said Sandra. And then they stood there, silently, facing each other. And Arthur came over.

"What's going on?" he said.

"There's been a fire outside," said John. "Something was burned out there. Something that was supposed to look like a green sports jacket." John held the bit of material out to Arthur. "Do you know what this is?"

Arthur looked at it, turned it over. "Can't say I do." There was a caution in his answer which made John turn from him in annoyance.

"I think you know what it is, Sandra. You do, don't you?"

And Sandra made a mistake. She shook her head and said, "No, I don't."

John said, "That does it. You have to know what it is. You wouldn't have to know how it got there."

Sandra repeated, "I don't know what it is."

155

John said, "Suppose I wanted to go to your room right now and search your closet."

Sandra said, "I'd rather you didn't." And she turned back again to Joanna and Lovechild.

"I think *you* know what it is," John said to Arthur. "I think you might as well admit it now. *She* knows what it is."

Arthur said, "Look. It's time you and I had a talk."

John said, "High time."

"Give me half an hour," said Arthur. "There's a man I have to see first."

"Where do you want to make it?" said John.

"My room," said Arthur. "I'll have some lunch sent up there. Perhaps I can get some Scotch out of my son. I think it's going to be a long talk."

"Very long," said John and looked from Arthur's retreating back to where Sandra stood across the lobby. And John shook his head and reached into his pocket again and fished around in it for a long while before withdrawing his hand. It was clear that whatever he brought out of his pocket was all that was in it and he stared down into his hand where a single .38 cartridge case lay.

It will be remembered—and if it isn't we are very kindly repeating it—that Gene August was not a well man when he arrived at Broadstone. He had come down for the sake of his nerves. Now, with three healthful days behind him he scarcely did more than leap from his chair and shout, *"What?"* when Arthur knocked at his door. August looked at Hutch standing on the threshold, watched him carefully close the door behind him.

156

"Mr. August," said Arthur, "you know who I am."

"You're God-damn right," said August. "You're the fellow who manages this steeplechase."

"I'm sorry, Mr. August. I know you haven't had the most restful time, but circumstances were rather out of our control."

The criminal lawyer grunted and then, being, despite his nervousness, a reasonable man, waved Arthur to a chair and indicated a box of cigars beside it. Arthur sank into the upholstery, picked up a cigar, and carefully took the cellophane from it.

"Mr. August, I have a business proposition for you."

"I am on vacation," said August.

"This is nothing you will have to do any work on now. Would you be interested in a criminal defense some time hence?"

"I might," said August. "What kind?"

"Will you accept the defense of the individual who will presently be accused of the murder of Merlin Broadstone?"

August squinted at him. "Who will that be?"

Arthur looked speculatively at the cigar and rubbed the fatty pocket under his right eye before replying. "I'd just as soon not say yet. I might be wrong. I mean I might be wrong about this person being accused."

"I don't accept cases without knowing who the accused is."

"No?" said Hutch. "Suppose you had to. This once. What would the fee be?"

"That depends on how important it is to you to get this person off and how much chance there is. What's the defense?"

157

"What would the fee be?" repeated Arthur.

August picked up a cigar. "You seem to have come in here with some pretty definite ideas. Maybe you ought to name it."

"Okay," said Arthur. "How's one hundred thousand dollars?"

August slowly bit the end off his cigar. "The way you say it it sounds more as if it were worth two hundred thousand dollars."

"I think you're wrong," said Arthur. "Could we settle at one hundred fifty?"

"Fair enough," said August. "What's the defense?"

"Insanity," said Arthur. "Temporary insanity."

"Was the person really temporarily insane?"

"Certainly not. Do you think I would be offering you one hundred and fifty thousand dollars in that event? This is somebody who must not be found guilty; somebody who's got to be gotten off on grounds of temporary insanity."

August rolled his cigar a couple of times in his moist lips and slowly put a match to it. "Well," he said, and puffed. "That's a pretty tough defense these days. Juries don't go for it." He puffed again. "However, is the person who is going to be accused of this murder anybody on this island?"

"Of course," said Arthur.

August took the cigar from his mouth, blew a satisfied stream of smoke across the room. "In that event I think we can do it. I may be wrong about this, but I am of the opinion that there isn't a single human being on this island

158

who couldn't be proven permanently, let alone temporarily, insane. Perhaps it would be politer if I were to say present company excepted."

Arthur held up a protesting hand.

"Don't do me any favors," he said.

ELEVEN

The Arthur Hutch who had faced Gene August was a man with his hair down. Clearly he knew, or thought he knew, the murderer of Merlin Broadstone. But the Arthur Hutch who called, "Come in!" when John Hugo knocked on his door half an hour later not only had his hair up but had it done in tight enigmatic coils.

"Sit down," he said. "Take it easy. I've ordered lunch."

"Thanks," said John.

"Care for a drink?" Arthur waved toward an unopened bottle of Scotch on the bureau. "I've got a couple more from where that came. I always said that son of mine must be good for something."

"You drinking?" asked John.

"If you do."

"Sure, why the hell not?" John went into the bathroom, returned with a couple of tumblers which he set on the bureau, and, picking up the bottle, peeled the wrapping from its cap.

"I told them to send up ice with the lunch," said Arthur. "But I'd just as soon have some straight now."

"I guess," said John. There was a resignation about

him—a tired, what-the-hell attitude. Something had happened to John Hugo when he found that bit of burned green cloth. Time was when nothing could have distracted him from the most precise attention to the case at hand. Now, he didn't even care if he drank on duty. Even for midnight, the drinks he poured would have been a bit stiff—and this was scarcely noon. He carried a glass across to Arthur, who reached up out of the overstuffed chair and took it in his pudgy fingers.

Arthur looked quizzically at the depth of the liquor, poutingly at John, and then shrugged. "How!" he said, and sipped daintily. John jerked his glass up in savage acknowledgment, gulped off half its contents, and coughed while agonized tears gathered in his eyes.

"Take it easy," said Arthur.

"Take it easy!" coughed John. "This is a fine time to be taking it easy. I've got an arrest to make."

"Oh?" said Arthur. "All wrapped up, huh?"

"Sure," said John. He banged his glass down on the table with what might have been meant to be assurance. But it came off as an overnervous gesture.

"Whom are you arresting?" said Arthur.

John met his gaze and then looked away. His eyes shifted about the room. He seemed to find nothing reassuring for them to rest upon. "Senator Drumbow," he said.

"That's interesting," said Arthur. "How do you figure it?"

John picked up the glass again and drained off the rest of its contents. "Don't you think it's pretty obvious?"

"Well, now," said Arthur, "you're the detective. You tell me."

161

"Didn't you have your ears open this morning?" There was a belligerence about John's tone which Arthur correctly recognized as a defense against uncertainty.

"Just when this morning," asked Arthur, "am I supposed to have had my ears open?"

"Up in Joyce's room, when that cockeyed oration was going on. You heard what Drumbow said. He said he hadn't liked Broadstone buying this island. He said he would have liked it better if Broadstone had bought that other place off the Southwest coast."

Arthur pulled at his ear. "Well, not exactly that. Drumbow said that he would have fared better if the island off his state had been bought and then, as I remember it, he turned to Joyce and said, 'You'd have fared better, too.' For that matter, I don't like this climate much either. I'd have fared better myself."

"Okay, okay," said John. "That's good enough, isn't it? That shows motive, doesn't it?"

Arthur looked into his glass ruminatively. When he lifted his gaze again he had a conciliatory expression on his face as if he would placate this young man, as if he were not eager to cross swords with him. "Let's skip that point for a minute. Assuming that he did have a motive, how do you figure he committed the murder?"

"Well," said John, "that's not too hard. Not too hard at all. Er—" He paused and looked at the bottle on the bureau. "Care for another one?"

"Not yet," said Arthur, "but go right ahead."

John poured a couple of ounces more into his glass—this time a little more slowly, like a man stalling while his thoughts raced. He sipped at the drink. "Take it like this.

162

Drumbow has this motive, like I just said. So he gets up yesterday morning early and he goes out of the hotel. He's got a gun. He goes over near the swimming pool—right at the corner of it, up against the blank wall, down at the end near the diving board. And he waits until he sees Merlin near the window of his room. And he shoots him."

"Wait a minute," said Arthur. "Those French windows were only open a little bit. If it had been fired from that angle, the bullet would have gone through the leaf on the right, and you know as well as I do that there wasn't a mark on that window."

"Doesn't mean a thing," said John. "Suppose Merlin wasn't standing right in front of the window. Suppose he was standing at the left side of the window, then the angle would be okay."

"Yes, sure," said Arthur. "Only the body was found square in front of the window."

"Well, think it through," said John. "Drumbow comes up to Merlin's room after he's killed him, and he wants to make it look as if the bullet came from the middle of the pool instead of from over at the edge of it. So he moves the body just so we'll think what we did think."

"And the pajamas?"

"That's the easiest part," said John. "He had to move the body, didn't he? Well, Merlin was a big guy. He had to drag that body. Dragging a bloody body would have left bloodstains. So naturally the first thing he does is put something on Merlin so the blood won't stain the floor while he drags him. The easiest thing to put on him is his pajamas. See? He puts the pajamas on him and then starts to drag. That's how the blood gets on the pajamas,

163

and through the pajamas to the floor. What's wrong with that?"

"I might," said Arthur, "be able to think of a number of things that are wrong with that, and then again maybe not. You know what I think we ought to do? I think we ought to go down the hall and tell it just that way to Drumbow and see what he has to say for himself."

For a young man who, a moment before, had announced his impatience to make an arrest, there was something undecided about John as he stood there absorbing Arthur's words. When he set his glass down it was the slowest motion he had yet made. "Okay," he said, "I guess maybe we'd better." And he said no more as Arthur levered himself out of the vast chair, or as the two of them walked slowly out of this room and down the corridor to Drumbow's.

Drumbow's door was partly open. They stood on the threshold until the Senator, who was looking moodily out of the window, sensed their presence, turned—startled for a moment—and then invited them in. Arthur closed the door behind them.

"Well," said the Senator, "have you arrested that double-crossing letter-stealer yet?"

John brushed this irrelevance aside. "Forget the letter. We got something more serious to talk to you about."

It might have been Southern courtliness or it might have been the action of a man stalling for time. But Drumbow rather graciously waved them to chairs. "Sit down, gentlemen. May I offer you a drink?"

"Certainly not," said John. "Never drink when I'm on a case." Arthur lowered himself into a chair, and indicated

164

to John that he had best do likewise. But John remained standing, stubbornly.

"Senator," said John. "Suppose I were to tell you that I think you shot Merlin Broadstone."

"Why, God Almighty, man, I did no such thing!"

"Sorry, Senator," said John. "But that's the way it seems to me."

"Looky here, son," said the Senator. "I didn't do it. How could I have done it? Why would I have done it? Have you gone crazy?"

Arthur bit the end off a fresh cigar and went on watching.

"Why you did it?" said John. "We heard you tell us that this morning. You said you would have been better off if Merlin had bought that other island."

"Well, sure. So what?"

"How much better off would you have been?"

"I did all right. I wasn't badly off at all."

"I asked you how much better off you would have been."

"You can't come in here asking me questions like that. Ain't you ever heard of Congressional immunity?"

"Take it easy, Senator," said Arthur. "Congress isn't in session. You're in the state of Florida now."

"You said it, I'm in the state of Florida. I never see a state like this. Out my way we're foursquare. We either accuse a man and lynch him or we let him go. I don't like all this nervous shilly-shally."

"Nevertheless, Senator," said Arthur, "I think you'd better tell the lieutenant how much better off you would have been."

"Well, sure, son," said Drumbow turning to John, "I'll

tell you that. Ain't no secret about it. You don't have to come barging in twisting my arm to make me tell you. The old so-and-so—I mean the deceased—said he was going to buy that there island in the Gulf off my state. So I buy a little property on the mainland, right opposite the island, thinking it'll go up in value—when they put in a ferry station. I weren't the only one that bought property either. Did you know your friend Joyce bought some there? Why don't you accuse him of the murder?"

"One thing at a time," said John. "Right now I'm trying to hear you get out of a murder rap."

"Well, Merlin Broadstone didn't buy the island. So the property I owned didn't go up in value. So I sold it. I even lost a little bit. Not enough to kill a man for."

"How much is enough to kill a man for?" asked John.

"Oh, about—er—" Drumbow paused. "What kind of question is that to ask! I'm tellin' you I didn't kill him. Anyway, I couldn't have. I was right here in my room the very minute the shot was fired."

"How do you know that?"

"I saw it, didn't I?"

John and Arthur said nothing.

The Senator came up from the window sill. "Damn," he said. "I didn't mean to tell you that. Looky here. Can you forget I said that?"

"Not likely, Senator," said Arthur. "You say you saw the shot?"

The Senator walked over to his bag, opened it, lifted a flask out, put it nervously to his lips and pulled at it. He banged the stopper back in and stuck the flask into his hip pocket.

166

"Yeah, I saw the shot. I was standin' at the window here. I saw it come right out of the pool."

"What time was that?" said John.

"Twenty of seven."

"Did you see anyone with a gun? Did you see where the flash came from?"

"I'm tellin' you I saw it come out of the pool. I didn't see anybody. Just the flash."

"Did you hear anything?" said Arthur.

"No, my window was closed. But I saw that gun flash coming right out of the pool. Who was under the water firin' I can't say. It wasn't that light, and the pool was still dark. I'll admit I hung around a bit at the window waitin' to see who would come out, but then I thought this ain't so smart. Because gun shootin' usually means trouble and I'm in no political position to get mixed up in any trouble. I hadn't even started to dress for breakfast yet, but if I was late for breakfast and there was trouble, first thing you know people would start askin' why was I late for breakfast. So after three or four minutes I quit lookin' and I got dressed."

"Three or four minutes!" said John. "How long do you think somebody can hold his breath under water? Whoever fired that shot would have had to come to the surface within a minute."

"Well now, son," said the Senator, "maybe you're neglectin' a thing or two about this murder case. You been down to the dock where they rent out the boats?"

"I landed there," said John. "What about it?"

"You haven't really looked around there much, have you?"

"Why should I have?"

"Because if you'd looked around there, son, you might-a seen those little helmets they rent out for folks who want to go down and wade around under water seein' fishes and shells and stuff. Fellow can put one of them on and stay down ten, fifteen minutes maybe."

John looked at Arthur with his mouth hanging open.

"Well, son," said the Senator, "speak up."

"Why didn't you tell us this before?" said John. "What sense was there keeping quiet about it?"

"Because I didn't want to get dragged into this damn thing. Because I can't afford being messed up in a murder case."

"Look here, Senator," said Arthur. "Maybe I can reassure you a little bit. The way these things go down here, it isn't likely there will be any trial until the middle of summer. When's Primary Day in your state?"

"June fifteenth," said the Senator.

"Okay," said Arthur. "Even if you're called as a witness —and you may not be—it mightn't be until after that. Now you'd better tell us exactly what you meant."

"I don't get it," said John. "You mean he sits here and doesn't say anything about this for two days just because of this election thing?"

"Take it easy, John," said Arthur. "It could be. And it's a nomination thing, not an election thing. For him that's big stuff. You know, Senator," said Arthur, "that story of yours isn't worth very much—about standing at your window and seeing the flash come out of the pool and it being twenty to seven. That's my son Carl's testimony, and most everybody on the island has heard it by

168

now. A little too easy for you to pick that up and use it yourself."

"Well, what do you expect?" said the Senator. "Expect me to turn up somebody who saw me at the window?"

"It would help," said John.

"Well, there ain't nobody. Unless maybe Mr. Joyce. He might have seen me."

"How could he have seen you?"

"Well, I saw him. Up there on the roof."

"You saw him *where?*"

"Up there," said Drumbow, and the two of them sprang to join him at the window and follow his pointing finger. "Right up there," said Drumbow. "On top of that there auditorium. He was standing there by the rail a minute and then he disappeared."

"When was that?" asked John. "Before or after the shot was fired? Before or after you saw that flash?"

"Why, it was before," said Drumbow.

"Then he would have had time," said John. "He would have had time to come downstairs to fire that shot."

"Oh, hell no," said the Senator. "Weren't more'n fifteen, twenty seconds before the shot. I just happened to be looking out and I saw his white suit up there. Then I looked down and the next thing I knew this whole big shootin' comes out of the pool—right straight out of the middle of the water."

John said, "So all right. You say you saw him up there. But that's no alibi."

Arthur pulled at his ear. "I'm not so sure, John. Just listen to your own case. You've got the murderer down there by the pool. If Drumbow was the murderer then he's

169

the one who's down there by the pool and up against the auditorium wall. In which case he wouldn't have been able to see Joyce on the roof above him. If Joyce really was on that roof, the only place Drumbow could have seen him from would have been from over here. Therefore if Joyce really was on that roof, Drumbow isn't the murderer. So it would seem that the next thing we do is ask Joyce if he was on the roof."

"You're damn right we do," said John. "And if he says he was, I'm going to ask him why, too, and why he didn't tell us."

The little lawyer closed his copy of *Reader's Digest* as John and Arthur came in.

"Hello, Daniel," said Arthur. "Got a few minutes?"

Joyce snorted and motioned with his magazine to his cast. "I've got six weeks. What's up now? Discovered another bastard of Merlin's?"

"Mr. Joyce," said John, "were you up on the roof of the auditorium at twenty minutes to seven yesterday morning?"

Joyce lowered his head and looked at John as if over the top of spectacles. "Well, young man, as a matter of fact, now that you mention it, I was."

"What were you doing there?"

"That's my business."

"Why didn't you tell us you were there?"

"I was protecting a client."

"How do you know it was twenty minutes of seven?"

"Actually I don't. I know it was close to that time. I know that when I thought it over later I figured I must have been up on that roof at just about the very minute that Merlin was killed."

"Can't you give us some idea of why you were up there?"

Joyce pouted at him. "Some idea? Sure. I was looking for certain notes I had made there the night before. I had been up there with a client, as I told you, and I made some notes in her behalf. Isn't it possible, young man, that we had better not pursue this line of inquiry?"

John glared at him. "What are you inferring?"

"You mean 'implying' and I'm not implying anything. I am saying flatly that on the night of Merlin's murder I was up on that roof with a client. I made some notes—"

"Pretty dark up there for note taking, wasn't it?"

"There was a moon. The next morning when I woke up, as I told you, my sinuses were playing hob with me. I went down, just as I told you, to the beach to get some salt water. Then I remembered the notes, so first I went up to the roof of the auditorium."

"Did you find the notes?"

"I did not."

"Were you in a position on the roof where you might have been seen by—well, to be frank about it, by Senator Drumbow?"

Joyce thought for a moment. "Drumbow? Where's his room? Across the hall?"

"Yeah, right over there."

"Sure," said Joyce. "If Drumbow said he saw me, he told the truth. I remember at one point, while looking for those notes, I came close to the railing. I even looked over the railing into the courtyard—thinking the notes might have blown down there."

"Then what did you do?"

"I left the roof."

"Right away?" asked John.

"You mean that instant? Well, hell's bells, no," said the lawyer. "I didn't fall through any trap door. I turned away from the railing and looked around for a minute or two more. I don't know how long. Then I came down to the auditorium lobby. And the man in the green coat attacked me. Previously I had told you that I'd been passing the lobby and heard sounds. That was not true. I said it because I wanted to leave out any reference to my coming down from the roof. Such reference would have—as it just has—led you to ask what I was doing there, and then I'd have had to tell you about the notes for my client—a fact, irrelevant to this case, which I preferred to leave undisclosed if possible."

There was doubt on John's face. And confusion, too. Joyce saw the expression and smiled sympathetically.

"I'm truly sorry, young man, that I had to mix things up for you. In telling you the earlier and somewhat, shall we say, 'abridged' story, I used my best judgment. The essential fact remains unchanged. I *was* in the lobby. I *was* attacked by a man in a green coat."

Arthur put a gentle hand on John's shoulder. "I'm afraid, my boy, that there goes your case against Drumbow. With Joyce where Drumbow said he saw him, then Drumbow couldn't have been where you thought he was."

"Yeah," said John. "That's true. But one thing, Mr. Joyce. A couple of times today something has been said about your having lost some money because Merlin

172

Broadstone didn't buy that other island—the one in the Southwest."

"Quite so," said Joyce, "I did."

"Much money?"

"Much? Depends on who you are. It wouldn't have been much for Merlin. It was a little too much for me. I think you heard about my losing this money from Drumbow, didn't you? I remember he said it this morning—or at least implied it—when they were all in this room."

"Yes," admitted John, "and he said it again."

"He is saying it a little too often to suit me," said Joyce. "I think I was fixed."

"How do you mean?"

"I mean that Drumbow introduced me to the man I bought that mainland property from. I'm pretty sure they were good friends. Drumbow claimed to have bought some himself. Maybe he did. But so help me, I think I was hornswoggled by Drumbow. I think he conspired to involve me in that deal. I can't prove it of course, but he may even have persuaded Merlin to pretend to have more interest in the island than he really had, to keep up the pretense of wanting it until Drumbow and his friend got me properly hooked."

"You were Mr. Broadstone's lawyer," protested John. "You must have known him a lot better than Drumbow did."

Joyce looked at him quietly. Then he said, "I sometimes wonder."

"Why? What makes you wonder?"

The lawyer shrugged. But he added nothing.

John sucked in a slow, long breath. "Okay, Mr. Joyce. I'll probably have more to ask you later."

"As a matter of fact," said Arthur, "there's something I'd like to ask you now, Daniel. When you were on the roof and looked over the rail into the courtyard, you were right above the pool, weren't you?"

"Sure. Right over it."

"You didn't notice anything strange about that pool by any chance, did you?"

"No, Arthur, not a thing. It was pretty dark down there."

John, at the door, paused and picked this up. "You mean the surface of the pool was dark? Too dark for you to see anything that might have been under it?"

Joyce thought a while. "I really don't know. It's hard to remember that. But it could have been."

And so John and Arthur were out in the corridor again, and heading for Arthur's room.

"We're running out of suspects too darn fast," said John.

They didn't reach Arthur's room right away. Another door midway down the same corridor stood partly open, and both of them were struck by the little tableau visible through the opening; so struck, indeed, that they stopped, opened the door further, and stood on the threshold, looking at Martha Lockhart and Sandra, at Lovechild and Joanna.

Sandra sat in a large chair, her eye-stopping legs flung over one arm of it. But Lovechild's eyes were not stopped by them. All of his attention was riveted on Joanna,

174

perched angularly on the window sill. Martha, as if chaperoning them, sat in a straight-backed chair and, like all chaperones, sewed or, rather, darned. And what she was darning was a sock.

"Why, come in, Arthur," she said. "And you, too, Lieutenant. We're just sitting here, talking."

Arthur advanced into the room, but John remained in the doorway, one hand against the jamb. His attitude was almost challenging.

"Still darning, Martha?" said Arthur gently. "I thought perhaps you were through with that now."

"Oh, no," said Martha brightly. "These are Lovechild's."

John snorted. "Who wears socks with a toga?"

Lovechild slewed his great head around. "I told you I don't always wear a toga. I wore those socks coming down here. I got a hole in one of them and Aunt Martha asked permission to darn it."

"My God, Sandra," said John. "Are you going to let your mother go into slavery for somebody else, now?"

Sandra swung her feet down to the floor and stood up, blazing. "She's happy. You let her be happy. She likes doing things for people. You wouldn't understand that."

John shook his head. "There's only one thing I want to understand. I'm asking you again, Sandra. Do you know what that thing was that was burned on the beach this morning?"

"I told you I don't."

"I know you told me," said John tiredly. "I wanted to give you a chance to take it back."

"You know what, Father?" broke in Joanna from the other side of the room. "Aunt Martha is going to teach me to darn."

"Dear Lord," said Arthur.

"And you know what else?" continued Joanna. "Lovechild has a wonderful idea. He thinks because of the way Uncle Merlin was killed, that it was done by somebody who was against health."

"You don't say?" said Arthur.

"Yes. He says there's a certain class of people who are against health, so naturally they'd want to kill Uncle Merlin who made so many people healthy. And he says it must have been somebody not very strong because he used a gun. He says a strong man doesn't have to use a gun to kill somebody."

"Uh-huh," said Arthur. "And what is this certain class of people which is against health?"

Lovechild, sitting on the floor, looked up at him. "Doctors," he said. "Founder was bad for doctors. If enough people had listened to Founder nobody would ever have been sick any more."

"What's more," said Joanna, "he says he has proof. He says he has a letter from Uncle Merlin about a time Uncle Merlin wanted to address a medical convention—the American Medical Association convention. What did you say he wanted to talk about, Lovechild?"

Lovechild looked at the ceiling as if the words were engraved there. "The Absolute and Final Cure of All Disease."

"That's right," said Martha. "And they wouldn't let him talk about that."

176

"You see?" said Joanna. "That proves it."

Arthur retreated toward the door. "It's very interesting. We'll bear it in mind. Let's get out of here, John."

But John didn't move at once. He stared at Sandra with pain and sorrow, with a sad tenderness masked by anger. And then he slowly slid his hand down the door jamb and turned and followed Arthur out of the room.

He should have waited a moment longer, for he would have seen Sandra's face dissolve in tears. He wouldn't have heard anything, though. For, as once before, her crying was soundless.

TWELVE

W<small>HEN</small> they had returned to his room and closed the
door behind them, it was Arthur who, for once, refilled the
glasses.

"My friend," he said, "I guess we have some more thinking and talking to do. Let's relax."

"Relax!" John almost shouted. "You can stand there
and say that. But do you know what kind of a spot I'm
in?"

Arthur blinked at him owlishly and then sank into the
big chair. "Sit down, friend. I really mean relax. Just sit
down."

John flung himself into a chair opposite Arthur with
such force that some of his drink sloshed out of his glass.

"You're in love, aren't you?" Arthur said.

"Sure. Of course I'm in love."

"You want to marry her, don't you?"

"What do you think?"

"I think you have the idea you can't. I think you have
the idea she's guilty. Come on, let's face it. You think
Sandra killed Merlin Broadstone, don't you?"

John bent forward and stared at his hands clasped

around his glass. "Do you think I want to think that? Why do you suppose I liked that case against Drumbow a few minutes ago? Why do you suppose I was ready to arrest him on what we both know wasn't any real sort of a case? I wanted to believe somebody else was guilty. For a minute there I had myself believing it really could have been Drumbow. All right. That's out. Maybe I could build up a case against some other people, but I haven't the heart to do it. It *has* to be Sandra. There isn't anybody else it could be."

Arthur blew cigar smoke slowly through his pursed lips. Then he said, "Maybe it would help if you told me what you think is the case against Sandra."

"The hell I will," said John. "I'm not sure I'll ever tell anyone that. I'm not sure I won't resign from the police force within the next hour. There are boats around here, you know, and she and I could get away."

"Oh, my God," said Arthur. "Is there no limit to your idiocy? I insist that you tell me what you think is the case against her."

"What for?"

"So that I can take it apart for you. So that I can knock it down."

"How do you know you can?"

"Because I know she didn't kill Merlin Broadstone."

"Then you must know who did kill him."

"Maybe. I'm not sure. But I know she didn't. I say again: You'd better tell me what you think is the case against her and let me beat it out of your head. And then maybe you and I can settle down to some really constructive thinking."

179

"Damn it to hell," said John, and he jumped out of the chair. "Did you ever see that girl in the swimming pool?"

"Uh-huh," Arthur nodded. "It's a sight that sometimes makes me doubt my avuncular detachment."

"Did you ever see her do that float of hers? Did you ever see her lie there, not moving a muscle, as if she were a raft?"

"Uh-huh."

"Have you ever seen anyone else around here who could do that? Is there anyone else on this island who could be in a swimming pool and yet not in it; who could hold a gun in a swimming pool and not get it wet; who could hold a gun in a swimming pool so still as to hit a target a couple of hundred yards away?"

"Okay," said Arthur. "That's point one. You think she's the only person on this island who could have fired that shot from the swimming pool. What's next?"

"What's next is we don't even need that floating stuff now that the Senator has come through with his little idea. Sandra must have known all about that diving equipment down at the dock. It would have been a cinch for her to take it and go down under the pool with it, holding the gun out of water above her head. Do you think there is anyone else on this island more at home under water than that girl?"

"Right," said Arthur. "I agree she could have used the diving equipment. But I don't agree that, with her eyes under water, she could have aimed the gun. However, what's the rest of your case?"

"Of all the people in Merlin Broadstone's will she was the one who needed money most. She needed it for her

180

mother. She made a fool deal with Daniel Joyce to sell her birthright for a mess of a few bucks. So naturally she regretted it and she had to act quickly before the new will could be written. After she had that conversation with Joyce she was the person who stood to gain more from Broadstone's immediate murder than anyone else in his will."

"Okay," said Arthur. "She had a motive. What else?"

"Daniel Joyce saw her. She was the person in the green coat that Daniel Joyce got hit by in the auditorium."

"How do you figure that?"

"Because she burned the jacket of her green suit."

"Oh? That bit of material you gave me was from a skirt."

"Sure. That's what we found. She had to burn the skirt, too. But it's a cinch she had to burn the jacket. Look, the minute I saw that green stuff I knew I'd seen it before. She had that skirt on the night she and I—she had that skirt on last night. It was wool, and it was part of a suit. We know that she burned it and then she tried to lie about it. Obviously there would be no reason for her to lie about burning her skirt. Except that if there was a green wool skirt there must have been a green wool jacket, too. If she was seen sometime wearing the skirt without the jacket, then someone might have realized that she could have been wearing the jacket with some other skirt the morning of the murder. So of course she had to burn the skirt because as long as the skirt was around it might have reminded somebody of the jacket."

"Okay," said Arthur. "Let's just take it from here. Are you contending that she was floating in the swimming pool

181

wearing the green jacket, or down under it wearing both the jacket and a diving helmet?"

"Listen, Mr. Hutch," said John. "I'm not kidding about this. There's nothing funny about this at all. Don't you see where the auditorium fits in? What's Daniel Joyce's story?"

"He had gone up on the auditorium roof. When he came down someone attacked him."

"You're damn right someone did. Sandra was there changing from a bathing suit back into her street clothes."

"Huh?"

"Yes, exactly. Look at her problem. She gets up the morning of the murder. She's got to get out of the hotel and into the swimming pool. If she puts on her bathing suit in her room she's apt to be seen walking through the hotel in it. And what's she going to say if somebody sees her doing that?"

"Well," said Arthur, "not to be too utterly brilliant about it, she might have said, 'I'm going for a swim in the pool.'"

John paused. "No," he said. "Damn it, that's no good. She had to have that gun. Look, Mr. Hutch. This you got to admit. When that girl is wearing a bathing suit there's no place she can hide a gun."

"True," said Arthur heartily.

"So she dresses in street clothes and she goes out of the hotel. She can't use the lockers and then go into the swimming pool because the lockers aren't open at that hour. So she carries the bathing suit in her handbag—and the gun."

Arthur smiled. But he didn't point out the paradox. If she were carrying a bag—

182

"She goes to the only place that's open and where she's sure no one will disturb her. She goes into the lobby of the auditorium and takes off her clothes." John paused and a shudder seemed to pass through him. "She puts on her bathing suit and comes around the auditorium into the hotel; she crosses some dark corner of the lobby and goes out into the courtyard. She gets into the swimming pool, waits till she sees Merlin Broadstone at his window, and shoots him. Then she goes back into the auditorium, gets out of her bathing suit and into her clothes. Before she can leave the auditorium, you know what happened."

"Sure," sighed Arthur, "an ash fell from her cigar onto the auditorium floor; you've analyzed it, proving it was hers."

John scornfully ignored this. "She was surprised there by Joyce. She springs on him before he can see her and knocks him down. That's easy, because Joyce is a little guy who probably doesn't weigh more than she does and he's nearly three times her age. When she runs out, all he sees is someone in a green jacket. She hides her bathing suit somewhere on the beach, throws her gun there, comes back into the hotel and gets the passkey from back of the desk. Nobody would pay any attention to her back there because she's a member of the family. She goes to Merlin's room, puts his pajamas on him to make the police think he was shot before he started to dress for the day. Then she hangs Merlin's key loosely on the inside of the door and uses the passkey to lock it from the outside. Then she returns the passkey and goes in to breakfast." He sat back wearily and rubbed his hand across his forehead. "Now do you see why I want to quit the force?"

"Yes," said Arthur. "I suspect because it isn't your kind of work. Would you mind answering a few questions? Suppose I'm the attorney for the defense. First I call my son, Carl Hutch, to the stand and I get him to testify to his having seen a flash come out of the pool. I then ask him if, at the time of seeing this flash, there was a beautiful curvaceous blonde, age twenty-three, floating in the swimming pool. Carl's answer will be that he did not notice any such individual. I will then produce on the stand in rapid succession some two hundred and fifty women between the ages of fourteen and forty all of whom will testify to the fact that they have been noticed by Carl under all conditions including extremely dark nights and at distances ranging up to three and a quarter miles. My question, in other words, is why didn't Carl see Sandra in the swimming pool?"

"That's too easy," said John. "Either she was under it, like Drumbow suggested, or else Carl did see her."

"How do you know?"

"Because I proved that she was there. So if she wasn't under water he had to see her."

"Why wouldn't he have said so?"

"Because he was protecting her. The same way she protected him twice in the last two days. 'This family sticks together,' she said. You're damn right it sticks together. What do you think you're doing right now if you're not protecting your own niece?"

"Okay," said Arthur. "My next question is that if Sandra could go down to the desk and get a passkey, why didn't she shoot him in his room? Why did she go through all this nonsense with bathing suits, green jackets, auditorium lobbies, and swimming pools?"

"Because somebody might have seen her going in or out of that room the morning of the murder. As long as she shot him from the swimming pool she could afford being seen going to his room later, because if she were seen then she could always prove that wasn't when the murder took place."

"Great," said Arthur. "Next question. To perform the shooting your way she would have had to be one of the world's crack shots. Now what makes you think she is?"

"What makes you think she isn't?" said John. "It's possible that there are several things she can do that you don't know anything about."

Arthur looked at him swiftly, but John was focusing out of the window. "And anyway," John went on, "how much of a crack shot would she have to be? All she had to do was hit the biggest man on the island. I think the question is how could she miss Merlin Broadstone?"

"Next question," said Arthur. "Here is a girl who, according to your story, is afraid to be seen going into Merlin Broadstone's room. But she isn't afraid to cross the courtyard and go into the swimming pool under the gaze of I don't know how many eyes at all the windows on three sides of this building."

"Not at all," said John. "She knew better than anyone else just what a strict discipline Merlin ran down here. She knew that, until the bells rang, nobody was going to get out of bed. The only thing she couldn't have figured was that one of the guests would be drunk and standing at the window. The answer was that only two people out of the hundreds here saw the flash. So she was reasonable in thinking that nobody would be looking out of the window. And then, finally," said John, "there's the clincher. What does a guilty woman do when she's afraid of being arrested?"

"I don't know," said Arthur. "What does she do?"

"She tries to make the detective. Look. I've been taken in. I am willing to stand here and admit I have been completely taken in—that I am hopelessly in love with this dame. But there's no getting away from the fact that she did it to me deliberately. That was her safety play. She wanted to tie me up in knots so that I wouldn't be able to do anything to her if I got wise. Well, God damn it, it worked." John walked over to the bureau and poured himself a drink.

"That's great," said Arthur. "That's just great. What are you going to do?"

"I don't know," said John. "I think I'm going to quit the force. I can't do anything else."

"And if you do, they'll put another man on the case, huh? And you'll have to turn over to him all the evidence you got."

"I suppose so," said John.

"And he'll probably come to the same conclusion you have."

"I don't see any other conclusion he can come to."

"In that event," said Arthur, "I think we'd better get together right now and solve this murder. Because you see I happen to be certain Sandra didn't commit it. I'm not saying I know who did. But I think we've got all the facts

186

we need. Are you willing to put this passionate prejudice of yours aside for a while and engage in a little pure reason with me?"

John walked across the room and stared from the window down toward the beach. Somebody knocked on the door. Arthur called, "Come in," and a waiter trundled a table into the room. All the while that the table was being adjusted, the places set, the dishes uncovered, John didn't move. Only after the door closed behind the waiter did he go to the table and absently pick up a celery stalk.

"All right," he said. "I'll play games."

"Fine," said Arthur. "First thing, sit down. Have something to eat."

"I'm not hungry," said John. And in truth he dallied with his lunch. The next twenty minutes passed wordlessly. Finally Arthur pushed back his chair.

"Look," he said. "I don't know where to begin on this. But you've been doing most of the detecting around here. Is there anything—anything at all—that's happened since you got on this island that you can't explain? For instance, how about that chisel that was thrown through the window in the next room? How does that fit in?"

"Easy," said John. "Sandra threw it. Carpenters are still working all over this hotel. She could easily have stolen a chisel. After she threw it, she was seen by Daniel Joyce in the green coat."

"Hah!" said Arthur. "I was at dinner that night. Sandra was down there. She was there through the whole dinner and she was there after you went upstairs."

"Was she?" said John. "She was up and around that smörgåsbord table a couple of times. How do you know she didn't leave the dining room and return? What's more, there was a scratch on the door jamb only about four feet from the floor. That happened when she raised the chisel over her shoulder to throw it. And it was that low because she's short."

"Nuts! Why would she have thrown the chisel into that room?"

"I don't know," said John. "Maybe there's somebody who suspects her and she was trying to get him. If I can believe she committed one murder, then"—he spread his hands sadly—"I can believe she tried to commit another."

"All right," said Arthur. "We've already got one small thing that doesn't quite fit. Come on now, what else has happened around here that you haven't been able to explain?"

"Plenty of things," said John. But he didn't get a chance to say what they were just then. The door burst open and Hester Hutch flung herself into the room.

"Hester," said Arthur, "we're just—" and then he stopped what was going to be a request for privacy. She was obviously disturbed beyond all reason. "What's the matter?" Arthur finished.

"You frightened Carl, that's what's the matter. The poor boy is all upset."

"What are you talking about?" said Arthur.

"Carl says you two are up here solving the case. He says he heard you say so in the lobby this morning. And he knows that you suspect him."

Arthur frowned and tried to shake a warning head at Hester, but John looked up with the eager attention of a man who has heard the suggestion of a reprieve.

188

"Why does he think we suspect him?" John asked.

"Because he says he found a bullet or a cartridge or something or other in the swimming pool and he doesn't think you believe he found it and he thinks that's what you're up here talking about. And he was saying some wild thing or other about your not thinking he had an alibi but that he did have one. And he says he's coming up here with his alibi. And I just wanted to get here first and tell you that if you suspect that boy or try to hatch up anything against him I'll—I'll—" She was unable to make clear what it was she was going to do, but there was that about her massive frame and the biceps she was flexing in her nervousness that made Arthur shudder.

"Listen, my muscle-bound pet," said Arthur. "You are now topping off a lifelong career of foolishness. We were not talking about Carl. There is nothing on the boy. There isn't a reason in the world to suspect him. That's right, John, isn't it?"

"Well," said John, "I suppose not—if he really has the alibi he's talking about."

"Alibi for what?" said Arthur.

"Well," John dissembled, "alibi—just an alibi."

"You see," said Arthur to Hester, "there wasn't a thing against Carl until you came into this room. Now you've given our policeman friend an idea; so of course he wants to hear this alibi and he'll do his damnedest to break it down and, no matter how innocent Carl is, if there's a loophole in that alibi we'll have real trouble."

"Oh, Arthur," said Hester, "I don't know how you can talk to me that way."

"Frankly," said Arthur, "I sometimes wonder how I can

189

talk to you any way. My personal preference would be to communicate with you solely by smoke signal." He paused as footsteps in the corridor halted in front of his door. "Come in," he called. "Come on in, you and your alibi."

A disturbed, distrait Carl entered. His alibi, while better to look at, was also nervous. Nancy, twisting her little bib of an apron, stood just behind him.

"Look here," said Carl, "I want to tell you I didn't do it."

"That's great," said Arthur. "I also would like to make a general announcement. I positively did not break into Fort Knox last night and steal the gold from it."

John paid no attention to this. He was carefully looking Carl over from head to foot and then, swinging his gaze to Nancy, doing the same job a little more slowly—in fact, pausing at certain strategic points.

"You didn't do what?" John asked. "Or perhaps, to save time, are you trying to tell us that you didn't kill Merlin Broadstone?"

"You're damn right I didn't kill him. What the hell would I have killed him for?"

"Well, for instance," said John, "two million dollars."

"I didn't know what I was in that will for and I didn't know how much the old so-and-so was worth."

"You didn't like him much, though, did you?"

"Oh, come off it, John," said Arthur. "If you're going to start accusing everybody who didn't like Merlin you'll spend the rest of your life at it."

"Okay," said John, and sat back in apparent relaxation. "Say, by the way," he said, "I have a hunch that a certain valuable piece of evidence has been hidden and I have an

190

idea it was hidden in the water—out in the Gulf somewhere. Would you know offhand," he said to Carl, "whether there's any spot off the island where the water would be at least eight or ten feet deep and the bottom would be dark, not sandy the way it is most places around here?"

Carl, relieved at this switch from himself, thought for a minute. "Well, sure," he said. "Out in the West Cove a couple of hundred yards offshore there's a patch of false coral—pretty big one, too."

"Oh," said John, "you've seen it? Rowed over it in a boat maybe?"

"Boat, hell!" said Carl. "I've walked on it."

"Walked on it!" said John. "How could you get down there and stay down long enough to do that?"

"Easy," Carl said, "we've got those little diving helmets—"

"Good enough," said John. "I was pretty sure you knew about those and pretty sure you were used to wearing them."

"What's up?" said Carl.

Arthur answered. "If you have alibis, my boy, prepare to shed them now. Our lieutenant friend now thinks he has you wrapped up. He thinks that at twenty minutes to seven yesterday morning you were wearing one of those helmets, standing on the bottom of the swimming pool, holding a gun above water, and shooting Merlin Broadstone. Now where were you at twenty of seven?"

"Right where I said I was," said Carl. "In my own room looking out the window."

"And your alibi?"

"For then?" said Carl. "I have no alibi for then."

"Oh, brother!" said Arthur. "What, in heaven's name, have you an alibi for?"

"The hour before that."

"And what's important about the hour before that?"

"Well, I can prove exactly where I was all night and right up to just a few minutes before twenty of seven when I was in my room. If I can prove that, then you got to admit I wouldn't have had time to be outside the hotel somewhere shooting somebody."

"Okay," said Arthur, "where were you?"

"Mother," said Carl, "will you leave the room?"

"Hah, that kind of alibi," said Arthur. "Don't bother going, Hester." He turned back to Carl. "I should think you'd be old enough to realize that I am going to be a lot more shocked by this alibi than your mother is. Now go ahead. Out with it."

"Well," said Carl, and then he stalled.

"Look, Mr. Hutch," said Nancy, "maybe I better say this. Carl and I are engaged."

"The hell you are!" said Arthur.

"A maid!" shrieked Hester.

"I am only a temporary maid," said Nancy. "I'm a movie star. That is, I'm going to be. Anyhow, Carl and I are engaged. We're in love, aren't we, Carl?"

"Yes," said Carl.

"And what," said Arthur, "has this to do with the hour before six-forty, as if I didn't know?"

"Well, Carl and I only got engaged that night and we had a few drinks in my room to celebrate. Only Carl had a few too many. You know how that is."

"Indeed I do," said Arthur.

"He had just enough too many," went on Nancy, "to get pretty sleepy. In fact he went to sleep. So I put him in my bed and I let him sleep there all night. And I sat in a chair and watched him."

It was possible that if Nancy ever got to Hollywood she would do pretty well, for somehow, as she told the story, around her there suddenly glowed the aura of Florence Nightingale, Clara Barton, and Whistler's mother.

"It was exactly twenty-two minutes of seven when he woke up and went upstairs to his room," she concluded.

"There," said Carl, "does that satisfy you?"

"I'm afraid not," said John. "She says she's in love with you, and somebody in love will do anything for the person he's in love with. Maybe it wasn't twenty-two minutes to seven. Maybe it was six-fifteen or six-thirty. If you two were going to get married what were you going to live on?"

"I can support a wife," said Carl. "I can work."

Not even Hester could hide her disbelief of this statement.

"Two million dollars would come in handy for a young couple setting out in life, huh?" said John.

"Well, suppose it would. I tell you I didn't kill him."

"Arthur," said Hester, "I've heard just about enough of this. Now I insist that you stop talking about Carl and arrest somebody else."

"As a matter of fact, my pachydermous pet, that is precisely what we were planning to do when you people came in and spoiled everything. Now if you will leave us alone again perhaps we can get down to business and," he

193

shook his finger at Hester, "don't come back into this room until we're out of it, and we may be in here for hours. If you need a room use Martha's. We don't want to be disturbed. As for you two"—he had turned toward Carl and Nancy—"I suppose there are things I could do in an attempt to block your marriage. I could, for instance, see to it that you don't get any of that two million for a long while. Under the will, you know, Carl, you don't get anything until after your mother dies. And let me assure you that she is in the pink of condition. However, and this may be addlepated of me, I am not minded to block your marriage. When I think of all the girls you might have married —and probably, had any of their fathers had the price of a shotgun, been forced to marry—your Nancy, here, begins to take on the appearance of the Woman Ideal. It could be, young lady, that, in a more profound sense than you are accustomed to use the verb, you'll be the making of Carl. Now get out of here and get to work. Do whatever you're supposed to be doing. Turn down some beds. No, don't do that. Do something else—anything else. But scram, the bunch of you!"

They scrammed.

THIRTEEN

Aʀᴛʜᴜʀ and John sat in silence for a few moments. At last Arthur spoke. "I must apologize," he said, "for my family. It seems to me that it is composed entirely of cretins. Yes, including my niece Sandra. It seems to me that she is the greatest fool of all."

"You don't say," said John. "It seems to me that she has acted with a great deal of cold, calculating intelligence."

"Nuts," said Arthur. "She never did anything sillier in her life than burn that skirt."

"She had to destroy it as evidence, didn't she?"

"Certainly not," said Arthur.

"Then why did she burn it?"

"That," said Arthur, "I'm beginning to understand. Look, my young friend, suppose you tell me who you think are the suspects in this case. Come on, name them."

John pushed up out of the chair and took his glass across to the bureau. "Have another one," he said.

"Sure," said Arthur and reached his own glass over. John poured doubles.

"Well," John said as he sampled his drink, "there's the

bunch with motives and that's primarily Sandra, Carl, Joanna, your wife, and Sandra's mother. In other words, everybody in the will. They've all got big motives. And Lovechild, too. Now there's the question of opportunity. It looked as if Drumbow had that. Maybe Joyce rules it out, and if Joyce does rule it out, it kind of rules out Joyce, too, because he couldn't have been seen by Drumbow up on the roof and shot Merlin at the same time. Almost anyone else might or mightn't have had opportunity. I'd say it comes down pretty much to the bunch in the will. Wouldn't you say so?"

Arthur didn't say anything. He took a larger swallow of his drink than he had heretofore, and when he put his glass down John had a momentary impression that his hand was shaking a little.

"There are some things," said Arthur, "that a man doesn't like to do. I'd rather not put the finger on the murderer for you. On the other hand I don't think there's going to be any stopping your finding out who it was."

"You're pretty sure you know who it was, aren't you?"

Arthur nodded his head. "Yes," he said. "I'm willing to tell you now that I am."

"Who?"

"I told you I'd rather you found out for yourself."

"At least, admit that I'm right when I say it's somebody in the will?"

"Yes," said Arthur, "it's somebody in the will. In a sense. But I'd like to remind you that you haven't named everybody who—in a sense—is in the will."

John looked at him, puzzled, and then suddenly sat up

196

straighter. "Good God!" he said, and there was admiration in his voice.

"Oh, you've got it?" said Arthur.

"Well, of course, you've told me. I must say I never heard of a situation like this before."

"Are you sure you know?" said Arthur.

"I'll describe him to you," said John. "You're telling me now that the murderer is a man who is not named directly in the will yet who stands to make a great deal out of it; a man, intimately connected with this family, who has recently shown that he is so close to it that he would go out of his way to help at least one of its younger members. You're telling me that it is an intelligent man who has been all over this case from the very beginning."

"That's right," said Arthur.

"But it's incredible," said John. "Don't you realize you're committing suicide? Why did you help me to it?" John snapped his fingers. "Oh, for crying out loud. And I nearly fell for it. You'd love to have me think it was you who killed Merlin, wouldn't you?"

"Would I?" asked Arthur.

"Well, of course you would. Because you really do think Carl's guilty. You know something I don't know about that boy of yours and you're trying to shield him. Well, forget it. There's no use making any grandstand play. All we got to do now is figure all the evidence against him. But it's a cinch that he's the guy we'll arrest before the day's over."

"Oh, hell," said Arthur, "evidently I'm really going to have to open your eyes for you. Before I do, I'd like you to know why I'm doing it. I'm doing it because Carl doesn't have an alibi and sooner or later you'll find it out."

"You mean that maid was lying?"

"I certainly do. But when I finish telling you how she was lying don't go rushing out of this room and start arresting anybody, because then we're going to have to sit down and solve this case—really solve it. That maid was lying when she said that Carl passed out in her room and she put him in bed and played nursemaid, sitting up beside him. Carl had been there with her and they'd gotten engaged as she said. As a matter of fact, even allowing for my son's boasting, I gather that they had gotten engaged quite thoroughly—three or four times, perhaps. And then Nancy made him leave her room because she had to go on duty in an hour and she wanted to be sure he was back in his room before he was due to be awakened by the bells. And he left her room and he started for his own and then he passed out. He passed out on the stairs. The service stairs. And he slept there for an hour or more. And he might have gone on sleeping all day if he hadn't heard a door slam somewhere below. And when he woke up he finally went to his room. So he doesn't have an alibi. So far as he knows, nobody saw him on the stairs."

"How do you know all this?" asked John.

"He told me, you idiot. He told me yesterday morning after I found those slippers in the bush and we walked off together. He was scared silly. That cock-and-bull story Nancy told was just a cover for him. You'd have found that out. You know how you'd have found it out?"

"No," said John, "how?"

"When you really started to investigate the murder. When you really started to cross-examine the murderer. Because he saw Carl on those stairs."

"How do you know?"

"He had to. I think there's one thing we can agree on. Every person remotely connected with this case has a room on the fourth floor. Right?"

"Right," said John.

"The murderer had to get outside the building. Right?"

"Right," said John.

"The murderer didn't dare go out through the lobby. The only other way was the back stairs. And Carl, somewhere on the back stairs between the ground floor and the fourth, heard a door slam at half past six. Right?"

John had stopped echoing. "So you say he says."

"That door," Arthur continued determinedly, "was being slammed by the murderer going out. And that means the murderer had passed Carl sleeping on the stairs. So"— Arthur leaned forward in a Churchillian gesture, fist on knee—"when you pin down the murderer, when you start cross-examining him, he's going to say that he saw Carl. The more he's trapped, the more he'll say it. He'll say it to implicate Carl; to prove that he wasn't the only person around the hotel yesterday morning who wasn't in his room where he belonged." Arthur sighed and relaxed. "God knows why, but I seem to have just enough fatherly feeling for that fool son of mine not to want him suspected of murder."

"I'm still suspecting him." John was dour.

"Yes, you are, aren't you?" Arthur drank from his half-filled glass. "You're suspecting him because in your

199

heart of hearts you're still sure Sandra did it. And you don't want it to be Sandra." Arthur waggled a finger at him. "Look what a fool Sandra's made of you by burning her skirt. That convinced you she was the murderer. So first you hope the criminal is Drumbow. Drumbow gives you a good argument and a chance to hope that it's Joyce. Now you're hoping that it's Carl. And all because you really hope it isn't Sandra. Well, suppose you stop hoping and start proving. And"—Arthur drank some more and cleared his throat authoritatively—"inasmuch as you haven't a chance of proving anything unless I help you, I insist on helping you right now. For instance, can't you see why Sandra burned her skirt? Can't you see the only real and legitimate reason she had?"

"Sure. I told you before that I could. And I wish to hell I couldn't."

"Open up your thinking, my boy. This morning when we were in Joyce's room and Drumbow was sounding off, you saw that envelope with those figures lying on the table, didn't you?"

"Yeah. Joanna dropped it there."

"Will you please stop concentrating on my children! Stick to the envelope. Did you see what happened to it?"

"I wondered about that," said John. "It disappeared."

"You're damn right it disappeared. Remember Joyce picked it up and shoved it into his magazine for a bookmark. Do you think a man of Joyce's intelligence needs a bookmark for the *Reader's Digest?* He knew it was evidence. Somehow Joanna had got hold of it, God knows how. So there is Joyce shoving evidence against him—"

"Against him?"

"Sure, sure. Only let's get to that later. We're talking about Sandra. So he shoves the envelope into his magazine and naturally Sandra burns her skirt."

"You don't say. Naturally, huh?"

"Of course. What was sticking out of the envelope? A laundry slip. Sandra knew it was her laundry slip. She recognized her handwriting. She thought Joyce was pulling that legerdemain to get rid of what he considered evidence against her. Sandra knew there was no evidence against her, but she had to figure from his actions that Joyce thought there was. Well, she sees Joyce doing something for her, so she decides to do something for him."

"Sandra suspected Joyce of the murder?"

"Certainly not. But she knew that he had twice told a story about a man in a green coat and there had been no evidence to support it. She decided to supply the evidence. 'Murderer Burns Green Coat to Escape Detection. Joyce Vindicated in Otherwise Unsupported Story.' That's why Sandra couldn't tell you that she knew what that piece of charred wool really was, because then she would have had to tell you why she burned it, and she didn't want to make you think she suspected Joyce. She was, of course, good and properly mad at you for immediately suspecting her. Oh, you've really played it smart."

"Me! How about her?" John was desperately determined that someone should appear even stupider than himself. Especially Sandra, at whom he was naturally furious for having allowed herself to be misjudged by him. "Why should she think she had to cover for Joyce? Who's suspecting him? He had no motive."

Arthur pulled at his drink and swallowed thoughtfully.

"But he did. I told you to open up your thinking. You have no idea how many people had motives for killing Merlin. Let's take Joyce, for instance. His motive's a honey." Arthur held out his glass and John rose to fill it, attending to his own at the same time. "Joyce fits a number of the specifications I mentioned before. Just to begin with, he is in the will and yet not named in it."

"How do you mean?" said John.

"I mean that he stands to benefit to the tune of a couple of hundred thousand dollars."

"Then you lied to me," said John. "You didn't tell me he was in the will for that."

"I did not lie to you. As a matter of fact both Joyce and I told you he was in the will, and if you had been thinking when we told you, you would have seen to what extent he was in it."

John lowered his glass and stared in vast confusion.

"Don't you remember," said Arthur, "that we told you that Joyce not only drew the will but that he was named in it as executor? How much do you think a lawyer gets when he puts an eight-million-dollar will through probate and then helps handle the estate afterwards?"

"Well, I don't know," said John. "I suppose he'd get whatever the family would pay him."

"True, and that would be quite a lot. But you're forgetting the question that Joyce asked me when I told him about Lovechild."

"What question?" said John. "I wasn't there."

"Right," said Arthur, "you weren't. I apologize. Then suppose I tell you that when I told Joyce all about encountering Lovechild on the beach and all about Love-

202

child's claim that Merlin was his father—suppose I told you that Joyce's first and only question was 'How old is Lovechild?' "

"Okay," said John, "you're telling me now. What about it?"

"My answer was 'He's twenty years old.' And Joyce pointed out that made Lovechild an infant under the law."

"Yo!" said John. "An infant!"

"That, it so happens, was also my reaction. I agree with you that in any sensible eyes that hunk of tissue and muscle is no infant. But in the eyes of the law he is. And when a will is probated and one of the beneficiaries is an infant, the whole probating process becomes vastly more complicated, and the probating judge, the surrogate, decides what the lawyer's fee will be. Customarily that fee is set by the court in terms of the size of the estate and the amount of executive work required of the lawyer in settling it. It is extremely unlikely that any judge would name for Joyce a fee smaller than two hundred thousand dollars in this particular instance. Frankly, it's my opinion that if the judge got a good look at this Broadstone family, he'd set the fee a lot higher. So Joyce was in for plenty of dough. Is that a motive?"

"I'm not so sure," said John. "To a successful lawyer, risking a murder rap probably wouldn't be worth a couple of hundred thousand dollars."

"Right," said Arthur. "This brings us to the next point. Was Joyce a successful lawyer? Or at least, was he at this point enjoying the usual economic fruits of success?" Arthur pushed out of his chair and filled his glass again.

"He was not. He had just lost his shirt in Southwestern real estate. Drumbow told you how Joyce had gotten hooked. Moreover did you see what was on that envelope which Joyce stuffed into his magazine?"

"Not very well. I got a sort of sideways glance. There were some figures, and I saw something about ferryboats. Something like that."

"Right. I saw it, too. You couldn't have known this, but that was Joyce's own handwriting. That was a computation of real estate and certain other deals. From what Drumbow told us, we now know that it was Joyce's own computation of how much he had gotten hooked for when Merlin decided not to buy the island in the Southwest and bought this one instead. Now Joyce was a pretty canny operator. As he said a little while ago, he wouldn't have bought that property out there if Merlin hadn't led him to believe that was where Broadstone was going to be erected. So Merlin must have changed his mind after Joyce had made the purchases and Joyce must have been burning up about that—whether or not he was also burning up about what he now claims was Drumbow's horn-swoggling of him." Arthur took another long drink. "You want any more motive?"

"If you give me much more," said John, "I'll arrest Drumbow for lying about Joyce being up on the roof." He waggled his head admiringly. Waggled it a bit more emphatically, perhaps, than a completely sober man would have. "You know, Arthur—you don't mind if I call you Arthur, do you?"

Arthur spread inviting palms. "Of course not, my boy.

204

Feel very warm toward you. You're a good fellow. Not smart, but a good fellow."

"You know, Arthur, if we worked out a few more cases like that we might hit the right one. Huh?"

"Might." Arthur was having some trouble with the cellophane on a fresh cigar. "Who'd you like a case against? Lovechild, maybe?"

"Oh, boy," said John, "that big stinker! Would I!"

"Don't think there could be, huh? Suppose your check of the air lines and boats doesn't turn Lovechild up. Suppose you couldn't prove when he came down. Then what?"

"Then it's still no good. We're still stuck with Grandpa's story. I phoned his grandpa up in Jersey. Grandpa says Lovechild was sitting right there in the farmhouse when the radio bulletin about Merlin came in. Rules him out."

"Why? We don't know anything about Grandpa. How do we know Grandpa didn't put Lovechild up to it? I mean up to coming down here and bumping off Merlin? Lot of money for Lovechild in that will. Could be a lot for Grandpa, too, then."

John seemed to poise himself for a trip across difficult syllables. "Accessory before the fact, huh?"

"Could be," said Arthur. "Look, want to hear the case?"

John meant to reply, "All right." But John was rather tight by now and what he actually said was, "Alri." Arthur, ordinarily acute of hearing, would have heard him say, "Alri," but Arthur, too, had consumed much and potent beverage. He wasn't really drunk, mind you, just tight enough so that "alri" sounded like "all right" to him.

Likewise, when Arthur answered, "Les take alla movs," John distinctly heard him say "Let's take all the motives." Consequently, though a sober eavesdropper would have had the greatest difficulty understanding the conversation which ensued, we will hear the words not as they were actually spoken, but rather as each of them thought they were spoken. Lucky us.

"What do you mean all the motives?" asked John. "Only need one. All the money."

"Better if there are more than one. There are. Look. First, as you say, there's all the money. He didn't necessarily know it was two million, but he'd know it was a lot. Okay, motive number two is vengeance. Merlin never made an honest woman out of Lovechild's mother, did he? After a while, Merlin doesn't even come around seeing her any more, does he? How do you think she liked that? Let me tell you something. I'm a lot older than you, see. No woman's going to be completely satisfied just being shot out of a cannon all her life. It may be exciting. I don't doubt it's even stimulating. But it's not the full life. Once she goes through the air and lands on the net, what the hell's she got until the next time they fire her? It's an empty life. Okay. The love of a son for his mother. It's a mighty strong motive. That's number two. Number three is—"

"Hey," said John. "This is good. You're really piling them up."

"Facts, all facts," said Arthur. "Okay. Here's Lovechild, a big, strong kid with a chance to be a world-beater

206

except for motive number three. What could Lovechild be a world-beater at? Physical culture. That's what. With all he learned from Merlin he could start an exercise cult, couldn't he?"

"Certainly could," agreed John amiably.

"Except for one thing. There is an exercise cult already. Merlin's cornered the whole God-damn exercise-cult market. But if he bumps Merlin off, he's got a clear field. How's that for a motive?"

"It's colossal!" said John. "Greatest little motive I ever heard. Let's have a drink on it."

"Good idea," said Arthur. "Glad you thought of it."

When John finished pouring there were two inches of whiskey in each tumbler.

"Now take the next point," said Arthur, setting his glass on the table next to him and making it on the second attempt. "Next point's Opportunity. He comes down here, maybe in a plane, maybe in a train. Doesn't matter how long ago he left Jersey. Grandpa will always give him an alibi. He doesn't have to come to the island in one of the regular boats. He can steal a rowboat and row over. With his shoulders and back that row is just a light workout for him. During the night, he hides down at the bottom of the service stairs. Come morning, he goes out. That's the door Carl hears slamming. He takes off his clothes and stands in pool. Right in the pool *with his nose out of water*."

"Huh!"

"Sure. The pool's nine feet deep at one end and less than four at the other. The bottom slants. So in the middle of the pool along one wall where the shot came from it's just about six feet deep. Lovechild's the one guy around here who could stand on the bottom with his nose and eyes out of water."

"Cripes!" said John. "That's wonderful. That proves it."

"There's more," said Arthur. "He's up against the east wall. The sun is rising behind him so he'd be in shadow. All Carl or Drumbow could see would be the flash."

John looked puzzled. "But Drumbow says he stood there for a few minutes after the flash and he didn't see anyone come out of the pool."

"Certainly not. Lovechild was looking up at Merlin's window. Drumbow's is very near it. He probably saw Drumbow and didn't dare move until Drumbow went away."

"It's terrific," said John. "Absolutely terrific. It fits at every point." He raised his glass. "My compliments to the duke." And then he stood there, holding his glass aloft. "Uh-uh. There's one little detail you're forgetting. Somebody came into Merlin's room after he was killed and put his pajamas on him."

"I'm not forgetting it," said Arthur. "The truth is, it's the only thing in this case I can't make head or tail of."

"Yeah," agreed John mournfully. "I can't figure it either." Then he brightened, as if two mysteries were somehow better than one. "Of course there's something else that doesn't make sense either. That conversation that Martha heard through Merlin's door the night before the murder when she wanted to put his socks away."

"I know," said Arthur, "she told me about that. Said Merlin sounded like someone on the Fred Allen show.

That's easy. Fits right into the Lovechild business."

"The hell it does. How?"

"Suppose Lovechild gets down here the night before the murder and calls up Merlin from the mainland. Suppose he tells him that unless he gets a lot of cash he's going to do him in. While they're talking Martha knocks on the door and Merlin calls out to her to go away. Lovechild, on the other end, wants to know what Merlin's talking about. So Merlin says, 'Somebody knocked,' and if the connection was bad and Lovechild didn't understand him he'd repeat, 'I say somebody knocked.' "

"Gee, that's wonderful," admired John. "It's the only possible explanation."

"The hell it is," said Arthur, offended. "Suppose Merlin had raised hell with Lovechild over the phone. Maybe he was sore that the kid had come down here. Then Lovechild gets real threatening and it dawns on Merlin that he's serious. Then Merlin has to get out of it; he has to laugh it off. So he says, 'It's a joke, son.' Remember Lovechild *was* his son."

Instead of being impressed by this additional display of virtuosity, John stared uneasily into his glass. "That doesn't explain one thing, though. How about that other stuff Martha says she heard through the door."

"Oh, yes," said Arthur. "How about that? Just what did she hear?"

John fished his notebook out of his hip pocket, moved it before his eyes until he achieved focus, and then flipped its pages. "Here. She says Merlin said 'for vegetarians' and then he said 'not rich Rotarians. Vegetarians.' What the hell does that add up to?"

"Gimme a drink," commanded Arthur.

"You bet." John went to the bureau and held the bottle up. "This one's nearly empty."

"There's another back of the bureau."

John braced one hand on the heavy piece of furniture and succeeded in snaring the new bottle in his other. "Wonderful Scotch, this. Very mild. I don't feel it a bit."

"Me either." Arthur was glaring at the dead cigar stump between his thumb and forefinger. "You know, Merlin was always talking about vegetarians. But I don't see why—wait a minute. Did he say '*for* vegetarians'?"

John handed him one of the two glasses he held. "That's what Martha said."

"For. Not of, not by, but for. That could fit. Suppose he was telling Lovechild that he couldn't give him any money, that he was setting up a foundation or something for vegetarians. It's just the crazy sort of thing Merlin would do."

"But why would Lovechild think he'd said 'rich Rotarians'? The connection couldn't have been that bad. Lovechild wasn't deaf."

"No, but Joyce was."

"Joyce? But I thought you said Lovechild—"

"I'm not saying anybody. We're just trying out different ideas. And Joyce is deaf."

"Not when he's wearing that ear phone."

"True. Except that Joyce told us that the morning of the murder he'd just put new batteries into it. Which means that the night before the murder the batteries must have been run down. So he wouldn't have been hearing so well."

210

"But what would Joyce have been doing in Merlin's room that night?"

"Keeping his promise to Sandra. Or even trying to do better than that." Arthur hunched forward in his chair. "Look. Sandra asked him to make a small cash settlement with Merlin for her mother. That wouldn't have appealed to Joyce. Maybe he went down to Merlin and tried to get a lot of cash for Martha—a real settlement, not the little one Sandra was after. Maybe Merlin said he couldn't afford it because his money is going into a foundation for vegetarians. 'Not rich Rotarians. Vegetarians.' See? So help me, it makes sense. Because Joyce isn't the kind of guy who would kill a man without first giving him a chance. I can't imagine Joyce killing Merlin for the two hundred thousand alone. Or to revenge himself for the raw deal in the Southwest—alone. But I can imagine him doing it rather than see Sandra sell her birthright. And I can especially imagine him doing it if Merlin is about to change his will, cutting out his rightful heirs and sticking in a bunch of lousy vegetable eaters." Arthur tried to bang at the table beside him but he missed. "I ask you. What the hell did George Bernard Shaw ever do for Merlin Broadstone?"

"I don't know," said John. "This whole case is too much for me. Can't we leave Shaw out of it?"

"Well, maybe," conceded Arthur.

"If it was Joyce in the room, how about that Fred Allen line?"

"Well, we've got that. If Joyce's ear phone wasn't working right, then when Martha knocks and Merlin turns around toward the door, Joyce would say, 'What's the matter?' And Merlin would say, 'Somebody knocked.' And Joyce, not hearing him clearly would say, 'What?' in his own ordinary voice, which wouldn't penetrate the door. And Merlin would repeat, 'I said somebody knocked.' And poor Martha would, of course, think of nothing except Senator Claghorne." Arthur drained off his drink. "There it is, my boy. Motive: a big slice of money. Motive: revenge for the raw deal Merlin pulled on him. Motive: effort to save Sandra from selling her birthright. Proof of the last of those: that he was in the room talking to Merlin the night before the murder, and Merlin was saying, in effect, no, no, my money goes for vegetarians."

Arthur pushed his cigar butt heavily against the bottom of his ash tray. "One other thing. We could build this case a bit higher. Suppose Merlin got angry at Joyce. Suppose he hit him. That would account for the big bruise on Joyce's face. He might easily have gotten that the night before the murder instead of the next morning in the auditorium."

"But not the broken leg," said John. "Couldn't have gotten that the night before."

"True. I'm just talking about that face of his. It was really hit. By someone with plenty of muscle and the know-how to use it. Remember what that mainland doctor said: that it's a wonder Joyce's cheekbone wasn't smashed. Merlin could have done that; and it would have made Joyce even madder at him."

Arthur stopped. And then he shot out a finger approximately at John. "And that would be the man in the green coat! Merlin was wearing a green coat—a green

212

pajama coat. They were emerald-green pajamas. At least that's what he had on the next morning. Maybe he was already in pajamas when Joyce was there the night before."

"He was," said John quietly.

"Huh?" Arthur was startled, as if the last thing he expected at any part of this case was confirmation.

"At least," retreated John, "he was always in his pajamas by that hour. That's what Martha said. Said when she came round with his darning he was always ready for bed."

Arthur spread his hand. "So. If all this is true a man in a green coat *did* hit Joyce. Just a few hours earlier, that's all."

John got up and filled his glass again. "Got to get Joyce off that roof," he said.

"Can't," said Arthur.

"Got to get him off the roof," said John. "Best case I ever heard." He returned to his chair, started to sit in it, hit the arm, caught the chair before it fell, and this time settled himself accurately in the seat.

Arthur leaned forward and waggled a slow forefinger at John. "Telling you. Can't get him off the roof. He's up there. Drumbow's a fool, but he's got eyes to see with. Drumbow says he saw Joyce up on the roof. He was there."

"Okay," said John. "Can you do it again?"

"Do what?"

"Build up another case like this. Somebody else. Somebody not on the roof. How about Bentley? 'Specially good if we could put it on Bentley. Couldn't lose down here. Republican Congressman. Couldn't stand up twenty minutes in front of Florida jury."

"No," said Arthur. "Won't wash. Got to make case with facts. You got the facts. Tell me. What's else in your notebook?"

John flipped its pages slowly. And shook his head. "Lot of stuff," he said, "but not important." He lowered the book and looked at Arthur, his lips pressed together, his brow furrowed. "There's one thing."

"Well?" asked Arthur.

"You're not going to like this," said John. "It's another detail that doesn't fit in. Nosir, you're not going to like it at all."

"What's that?" asked Arthur.

"Why'd Carl pick my pocket?"

FOURTEEN

THE question John had asked must hang, menacing and unanswered, for a few moments while we turn to another facet of this many-sided case. The management regrets these interruptions; it is merely making every effort to leave no fascinating episode undescribed.

For instance, if—a little later in this record—we were to take you to Carl's room and show you Drumbow unconscious on the bed, Nancy lighting a fire on the window sill, Carl cowering behind the bureau, and Bentley, in the bathroom, bathing his face in bloody water, you might wonder. You might even complain to the management about its omission of essential details. It is better, therefore, to interrupt John and Arthur now, shift our focus a bit, and give you the few, simple facts leading up to the carnage in Carl's room.

The whole thing was just one of those perfectly forgivable misunderstandings which is bound to occur at some time or other among any little group of earnest thinkers.

It began with a kiss. A chaste kiss. Lovechild, shortly after he and Joanna had left Martha's room, no longer able to restrain the mighty waves of passion piling up within him, had taken Joanna's head in his huge paws and, fighting grimly but hopelessly against his baser nature, kissed her on the forehead. Then, realizing the gross and brutal thing he had done, he'd flung an arm across his eyes and stumbled blindly away, leaving Joanna exulting at the purity and general excellence of this young man who loved her.

Joanna's next thought was not so exultant. Her own character was nowhere near as pure or excellent as his, and if he discovered this, his disappointment in her would be terrible and, probably, irremediable. *And right in this hotel, in her brother Carl's possession, was a letter which proved her lack of total purity.* She had to get that letter and destroy it!

At once, she began a frantic search for Carl. She found him, presently, crossing the lobby, carrying a loosely wrapped package which he had just taken from the rear of the station wagon outside.

"Carl!"

He looked at her dreamily, a betrothed young man still savoring his father's recently given blessing.

"Carl!" she repeated. "I've got to have that letter. Right away. Where is it?"

"Letter?" dreamed Carl. "What letter?"

Joanna mistook his Nirvana-state for a stall. "You know damn well what letter. You give it to me or I'll turn that Nancy of yours over to the police."

This shook Carl out of the clouds. "You can't; she hasn't done anything."

"Oh, no?" Joanna quickly pressed home the point that

216

was so obviously scoring. "How about her stealing evidence from the fourth-floor rooms?"

Carl was suddenly aware that the lobby was a public place. "Let's get out of here," he whispered, and seizing her arm rushed her toward an elevator.

But his precaution was too late. Congressman Bentley, lurking near the desk, had eavesdropped. He couldn't hear all that was said. But it was necessary for him to hear only the word "letter." Instantly he was in another elevator.

"Follow that car!" he hoarsely commanded the operator, pressing a dollar into his hand and motioning toward the adjoining elevator shaft. They shot upward, the operator watching through the fan hole in the car's roof the reflected lights of the other elevator. When Bentley emerged in the fourth-floor corridor, Joanna and Carl were still visible near its end and heading for Carl's room. When they entered it and closed the door behind them, only another moment elapsed before Bentley had his ear to the door.

He heard the main outlines of the drama. Joanna demanded the letter, almost tearfully admitted that she wanted only to destroy it, confessed her love for Lovechild, then, anger mixing with her tears, repeated her threat to tell the police how Nancy had stolen evidence from the wastebaskets and withheld that evidence. He heard Carl deny that the trash was evidence, object violently to the idea of his sister marrying what he termed "that gorilla," threaten to turn the letter over to Bentley, in whose hands it would do the most public harm. Mightily

217

cheered, Bentley was raising his knuckles to knock on the door and receive the letter when a door opened up the hall and Bentley saw Drumbow emerge from it. Not wishing to lead Drumbow to the treasure, he turned from the door and pretended to have had no interest in it. But not in time. Drumbow had seen the raised hand and then the sudden decision not to knock, correctly surmised that this decision had to do with his appearance in the hall, and came striding down it to investigate. Ignoring Bentley, who was powerless to do more than stand there and watch him, Drumbow applied his ear to the door. Both Joanna and Carl belonged to that school of argument which attempts to win by the device of endless repetition. Thus Drumbow heard all that Bentley had. And more. For now Joanna had begun to search the room. The opening and closing of drawers mingled with the sounds of slapping and scuffling. The drama was drawing to a climax. The slaps, let it be said for Carl, were all of that lighter variety which marked them as delivered by Joanna. But suddenly one of them was followed by a thwack. Exactly the kind of thwack one achieves by using a male palm to strike a thinly covered female buttock. From out the room came Joanna's suddenly strident voice:

"*You beast!*"

Nancy, tidying Lovechild's room, heard it. So did Lovechild. Like a great bull-elephant trumpeting to the rescue of its mate, Lovechild went charging from his room and down the hall. Nancy, never the girl to miss fun and games, followed. Lovechild accurately estimated the direction from which the sound had come and confirmed it by the attitudes of Bentley and Drumbow, tense before Carl's

218

door. Never hesitating, Lovechild careened down the hall and spurning doorknobs hurled himself through the door. The room, being thus conveniently opened, Bentley, Drumbow, and Nancy entered, too.

Carl had not gained the second flight of tennis players without the possession of fast reflexes and a nimble body. Even as the door tumbled in and Lovechild's frame became visible, Carl made a headlong dive which took him behind the bureau and out of sight. Lovechild flung a protecting arm around Joanna and inquired in a foghorn bellow who was molesting her. Joanna, seeing the Senator and Congressman come in, and filled with the sense of their general embroilment of her, pointed accusingly at them both. Lovechild swung once to Drumbow's chin, once again to Bentley's nose, and then, arm in arm, he and Joanna stepped over the debris and into the dawn of a better day. Joanna passed Nancy on the threshold and, desperately needing her assistance, addressed her with well-calculated affection.

"Hello, sis."

And Nancy nearly cried. It was so wonderful of this girl thus to welcome her into her famous and—from where Nancy stood—practically noble family.

"Hello," said Nancy.

And then Joanna bent and whispered in Nancy's ear. And Nancy nodded, happy to have something to do for this patrician girl. "Sure, kid," she said. "I know where it is. Leave it to me. I'll burn it."

See? That's all that happened. Now we can get back to where John had said to Arthur, "Why'd Carl pick my pocket?"

FIFTEEN

Go on!" said Arthur. "Carl's no pickpocket. Too clumsy."

"That's what you think. That's what I thought, too. But he isn't. He did." John tried to put his hand into his pocket; missed twice while his hand slipped down the side of his pants. On the third try he made it and from his pocket he pulled out a small object which he tossed on the table. "See that?" he said. It was the cartridge case of the .38 bullet. "It's been in my pocket since I found it. Found it yesterday. Not what Carl says. He says he took it out of the swimming pool this morning." John slipped his hand down on the arm of his chair. "Couldn't have. There weren't two shots fired. There weren't two bullets. Couldn't have been two cartridge cases. Just one. Don't know why he did it. But he took it. Right out of my pocket. Then he pretends he found it in the swimming pool and gives it back to me."

"It's a serious charge," hissed Arthur. "Also, it makes no sense. If Carl were the murderer, he might have taken the cartridge case to suppress evidence. But then he wouldn't give it back. No sense at all." Arthur moved his

220

glass on the table next to him and rubbed with a pudgy finger at the little exposed wet ring. "When'd you last know for sure you had the cartridge case? When were you last sure it was in your pocket before Carl found it in the pool?"

"This morning," said John. "Up on the roof. You were introducing Lovechild. I was standing with my hands in my pockets and I had that thing right in my fingers."

"Okay, okay," said Arthur. "Then Carl couldn't have picked your pocket. He was down in the swimming pool."

"That's what he says. Maybe he was up on the roof first. Pretty big crowd there. Could've been there without my knowing it. Anyway, fact is he had it a few minutes later. Gave it to me in the lobby."

"What did you do on roof?" asked Arthur.

"Nothing," said John. "Just up there."

"Oh, no," said Arthur, and he waggled a finger at John. "Not telling the truth. I saw you. You took the exercises. Took them right along with all the others."

"Oh, that," said John. "So what? I took the exercises. Thought it would be fun. Wasn't. Just dull. Gives you a crick in the back."

"Okay," said Arthur. "You took the exercises. How'd you know the cartridge thing didn't fall out of your pocket? Maybe you were jumping up and down or something."

"Well, I don't know," said John. "Suppose it could have. But then it would have landed on the roof. Carl would have found it on the roof. Why did he say he found it in the swimming pool?"

"I dunno," said Arthur again. "Interesting question. Let's try to figure when it could have fallen out of your pocket up on the roof. What would have been the most likely time? Doubt that business of coming out of your pocket while you're jumping up and down."

John concentrated on an attempt to light a cigarette while holding his glass in one hand. "Well, maybe it was while I was lying on my back. Doing that cockeyed exercise. You know, this one." And John, putting down his glass, struggled to his feet, with elaborate care moved a chair out of the way, and, with even greater care, lay down on his back on the floor.

Slowly John raised both feet into the air, raised them until they pointed at the ceiling, let them go on back, back, over his head until his toes touched the floor. "Like this." Then he tried to lift his feet away from the floor again but it was a little too much for him in his present condition. "I'm stuck," he muttered.

Arthur got to his feet, but not to help him. He stood looking down at John—looking at him with a suddenly well-focused gaze. It was as if he had been struck so forcibly by an idea that inebriation had been driven from him.

There was John: his head, his neck, the upper half of his back pressed close to the floor. There was the small of his back lifted away from the floor, lifted away, indeed, from the back of his coat, which remained lying on the floor. There were his buttocks pointing at an angle midway between floor and ceiling. There were his legs stretched across his chest and his face, his knees tousling his hair, his toes on the floor.

"Hold it," said Arthur, and went over and rummaged in his desk. He came back and bent over John and suddenly John said, "Ouch! Whaddya doing to me?"

Arthur said nothing. Then John felt his legs being pushed away from his face, saw Arthur's extended hand, took it and was helped back to his unsteady feet.

"Sit down, friend," said Arthur, "back in a minute."

Arthur went into the bathroom. John, craning round, saw him remove coat and tie, flood cold water from the basin faucet and—with only a slight shudder—stick his head under it. Time and again he ducked himself. Once he toweled roughly, came into the bedroom and poured coffee from the thermos on the luncheon table. He gulped this off and returned to the bathroom for more sluicing. It was the deliberate act of an intelligent man who was determined to get sober no matter how much it hurt. And it worked. But this was not enough for Arthur. Imperiously, he stood in the bathroom door and summoned John. And John, like an about-to-be-bathed puppy, went. The whole thing took nearly twenty minutes. A lot of water went down the drain. A lot of coffee went down their throats. At the end of it they faced each other, red-eyed, shaking a little, but—for the moment, and for the most part—sober.

"How do you feel?" said Arthur.

"Okay," said John. "Except for that damn exercise I did before. Whatever made me do that?"

"I don't know what made you do it," said Arthur, "but I think in a few minutes you'll consider it the finest piece of police work you ever tried. You, young man, have solved the murder of Merlin Broadstone."

"I have?" said John.

"Yep. Now you got to listen carefully and we got to take it step by step. You said the only time the cartridge

223

case could have rolled out of your pocket was the time you were lying on your back and doing the exercise. I agree with you. That's when it did roll out of your pocket."

"So what?" said John. "So it rolls out of my pocket then. But that leaves it on the roof and that son of yours, what does he say? He says he found it in the swimming pool. How could it have gotten in the pool? Remember, there's a wall around that roof, a brick wall all around, and about four feet high."

"That's right," said Arthur. "There's a brick wall around that roof. Now what do you think happens when it rains?"

John pondered for a moment. "That's easy," he said, "the roof gets wet."

"Sure," said Arthur. "It gets wet, but it doesn't get flooded. You've lived in Florida a long while, I gather. Do you think we'd have come down here and built a hotel without taking a precaution against such a familiar Florida phenomenon—" Arthur paused and shook his head in self-admiration, "greatest piece of sobering up I ever did in my life—such a familiar Florida phenomenon," he repeated proudly, "as a Florida hurricane? When we put this hotel up don't you think we realized that as much as two or three inches of rain might fall in a single hour? Don't you think we provided for the drainage of that roof?"

"So?" said John.

"So if you go up and take a look at that brick wall again you'll see that every few feet along its base there's a brick missing. That's for the rain to run out. We wouldn't care how wet the courtyard got. Now you listen to me. If that cartridge case fell out of your pocket on the roof, then it had to go through one of those holes in the wall because the roof slopes that way. And if it went through one of the holes above the swimming pool it would have gone into the pool. Capable as my son is of stretching the truth now and then, I think he was giving it to you straight this morning. He found that cartridge case in the pool just as he said."

John shrugged. "Well, maybe. So what? So he didn't pick my pocket. But that doesn't solve the murder like you said I just did."

"Take it easy," said Arthur. "How do you know that this morning was the first time that cartridge case fell from the roof? How do you know it didn't do the same thing on the morning of the murder?"

"Oh, for crying out loud," said John, "you're trying to pin it on Joyce again now."

"No," said Arthur. "I'm not trying to pin it on anybody now. It's pinned."

"But why make the case tougher?" said John. "We're having trouble enough. If the guy was shot from the swimming pool then how could the cartridge case have fallen from the roof?"

"Look," said Arthur. "Merlin's room is on the fourth floor, right?"

"So?" said John.

"And this is an eight-story building. Right?"

"So?" said John.

"So the angle from the roof down to Merlin's room is exactly the same as the angle from the courtyard up to Merlin's room."

"Oh?" said John.

"Yes, oh," said Arthur. "I'm suggesting to you that Merlin might have been shot from up on the roof instead of from down in the courtyard."

John's unsteady hand swept Arthur's words aside. "For-

225

getting something. Forgetting bullet went into small of
Merlin's back. Ended up in Merlin's heart. Bullet traveled
up in his body."

"Put your hand in your pocket," said Arthur.

This time John made it on the first try.

"Touch the bottom of your pocket."

"Okay," said John.

"Okay," said Arthur. "Which is higher, the bottom of
your pocket or the opening of your pocket?"

"What are you talking about?" said John. "Opening,
of course."

"Fine. Yet you just admitted that when you were exercising this morning, the cartridge case could have rolled
out of your pocket. Things can't roll up. They only roll
down. So when you were in that position on the floor, the
bottom of your pocket was higher than the opening."

"You trying to tell me somebody shot Merlin when he
was standing on his head?"

"Of course not. I'm trying to tell you that Merlin was
shot while he was exercising. Dear God, if there's any one
thing that's all over this case it's exercise. This whole
blasted island is dedicated to exercise. Except for me, there
isn't a single person here who doesn't live and breathe for
exercise. What do you think these people do when they
get up in the morning, even before they brush their teeth?
I'll tell you. They exercise. They do setting-up exercises in
their rooms. Didn't you hear that the first mass exercises
are held after breakfast, but that everybody does calisthenics in his room before? And if you don't know it, I can
tell you. Because I've been married to a woman who has
gotten up and exercised every damn morning since our

226

honeymoon. Even on our honeymoon. Made me feel like a fool. What do you think Merlin did when he got up that morning? He went to his partly open window and he breathed in and he breathed out. And he flapped his arms and he touched his toes. And then, my poor fool, he went down on his back with his feet toward the window and he raised his feet in the air and he brought his feet up over his head and touched them to the floor behind his head. Now, my young friend, John, I submit to you that if at that moment somebody standing on the roof had fired a bullet through Merlin's window, that bullet would have hit him in the small of his back—which was the highest part of his body—gone part way down through his body, and ended up in his heart, which, in that particular position, was a damn sight lower than the small of his back. Then what would have happened? His legs would have come flying down, and he would have ended up stretched on the floor with a bullet hole in the small of his back and a bullet in his heart—a perfect picture of a man who had been shot from below. And look what else happens," said Arthur, "when his feet come flying down, his slippers go catapulting off just as if they had been shot from a sling. They sail right out through the window and Carl sees a couple of brown things descend and land in that damn bush."

"Wait a minute," said John. "Jus' a minute. If what you're saying now is true, then Carl's lying. Carl's lying when he says he saw a flash come out of the pool."

Arthur grunted, stared at the floor for a few moments. Then he banged his hand on the table. "The hell he was lying. He did see the flash come out of the pool. Do you

227

know what a swimming pool is on a windless morning? It's a mirror. He saw the reflection of the flash in the pool. And that's the same thing Drumbow saw. What did Drumbow say he saw first? He said he saw Joyce on the roof and then he says Joyce disappeared. You bet you Joyce disappeared. He didn't want to be seen by anybody up on that roof firing that gun. He got down on his belly on the roof and he looked through one of those drainage holes where the brick's missing, and he stuck his gun through it and he fired just at the moment that Merlin was in the only position that would seem to have ruled out any possibility of the shot having come from anywhere except below. The minute the bullet was fired, the cartridge case fell to the roof, rolled out the little opening, and fell into the pool. Merlin, instantly killed, collapses. The feet come flopping down. The slippers go sailing off. The pajama legs stay bunched up toward his knees, the way they were when I found him. And what does Joyce do? I'll tell you what he does. He crawls to the other side of the roof, and he stands up. He can stand up safely there because nobody in the hotel can see him when he's on the other side of the roof. He's got to get rid of the gun, so he throws it away. He doesn't care where it lands as long as it lands somewhere where it can't be tied up to him. Well, where would a gun land if you threw it off the roof from the side away from the courtyard? It would land on the beach, which is exactly where you and Sandra found it. That's the case. Let me give it to you. Joyce, needing money, certain of getting a big fee for probating the will, furious at Merlin for welshing on the other island deal, determined to save

Sandra from selling her birthright, goes to Merlin's room the night before the murder, tries to argue him into a big settlement for Sandra. He learns from Merlin of Merlin's plan to give a lot of money to some foundation or other for vegetarians. He doesn't hear Martha knock on the door. He finally hears Merlin telling him, 'Somebody knocked— I say, somebody knocked.' Some time after that, having gotten nowhere with Merlin, but having been hit a terrific blow by Merlin's fist, he leaves the room determined to kill him. The next morning he dresses, goes down the corridor, down the service stairs, tiptoes past Carl, lets the outer door slam behind him, goes around the hotel on the outside, into the auditorium, climbs eight flights to the roof, to avoid going up in a hotel elevator where he would be seen or walking up hotel stairs where he might be seen, is nevertheless seen for a moment by Drumbow up there, then gets down behind the wall and sights at Merlin's room through one of the holes in the wall, watches Merlin take his exercises—waiting for the one exercise he knows Merlin is bound to include—and shoots him at the moment that Merlin is upside down. Haven't you wondered why nobody heard the shot? If it had been fired in the courtyard, the whole hotel would have heard it. But fired from the roof, and inside the wall of the roof, the sound was bounced *up* and away from the hotel. After he fires, Joyce goes to the other side, throws the gun from the roof, and then he goes downstairs. And what happens while he goes downstairs? Is he in a hurry? You bet he's in a hurry. He wants to get back into that hotel and up to his room so that when the bells ring for breakfast he can be seen coming out of his

229

room as if he had just gotten up. So coming down those stairs in a hurry—particularly that last curving flight into the lobby—he slips. And then what happens to him? He breaks his leg.

"Was there a man in a green coat? Of course not. Except for Merlin, the man in the green pajama coat, who had hit him the night before. It was an invention that he had to make up in order to explain his presence in the auditorium and his broken leg. Being a smart guy, he invents a mysterious and sinister figure in the hope that figure will be suspected of being the murderer. From then on he sits in his room with a broken leg. But he's not immobilized. He's in a wheel chair which he can move around very easily. He's got to do something to cinch the case against the mysterious man in the green coat. So he steals a chisel from one of the carpenters, who, as you observed, are working all over the hotel. Then he gets Hester on the telephone in his room. He gets her to read something over the phone. When you're reading something, when you're doing all the talking the way Hester was, you can't be sure whether the person on the other end is listening or not. Daniel wasn't listening. He wasn't even on the other end. Look how easy it was for him to put the receiver down on the table, wheel himself into the corridor, throw that chisel into an empty room—maybe he wanted it to go through the window, maybe he didn't. And you bet the scratch on that door jamb was low; the thrower of that chisel was *sitting!* Now he wheels back into his own room to hear Hester saying, 'What was that noise?' and what does he do? He pretends that he has seen the man in the green coat, that he's in a great fright. A man in a green coat has again appeared—but only to Joyce—and again has done something sinister. That's the case, and there's only one thing I don't like about it. I don't like the fact that Joyce is ten times the human being that Merlin ever was; that Merlin was a selfish fanatic, and that Joyce—until his need for money and his sense of revenge got too much for him—was a decent little guy. But I'll tell you this. I don't care what you think. My own opinion is that Joyce would never have committed that murder if it hadn't been to save Sandra. I've heard of worse motives in my life. I mean I've heard of motives that were a lot meaner than that, and so have you."

John slowly stood up, shook his head as if trying to clear it. "I guess that's it," he said. "But I don't see how we'll ever take it into court until we get that business about the pajamas. Why did Joyce go into Merlin's room afterwards and put his pajamas on him? Why?"

"He didn't," said Arthur. "Nobody went into Merlin's room from the minute he was shot until the minute Sandra and I went into it and discovered the body."

"But then how—"

"Go into the bathroom," said Arthur. "Take a look at the mirror on that door. Now turn around. Take a look at the back of your coat at the same point where the bullet hit Merlin."

John stood there, swaying a little in front of the mirror, his head twisted over his shoulders, with a great effort focusing his eyes on the mirror. "Well, I'm looking," he said. "There's nothing on my coat."

"You bet there isn't," said Arthur. "Now lift up the back of your coat. Go on, lift it up high. I want you to look at your shirt at the same spot."

John hiked up the skirt of his coat until it was gathered across the middle of his back.

"Hey," he said. "I got some ink on my shirt. How the hell did that happen?"

"I put it there," said Arthur. "I put it there while you were lying on the floor with your feet over your head. I went over to my desk and got my fountain pen and I scratched that ink right on your shirt. That's when you wondered what I was doing to you. You know where your coat was when I was doing that? The skirt of it was lying on the floor. Just the way a loose pajama coat would lie on the floor when you raise your body up and away from it. That's why there was no bullet hole in the pajamas. That's why there was only blood—blood that got on the pajama coat after Merlin's body had collapsed, his feet had come down, and he lay there bleeding."

Throughout these final words Arthur had been sitting forward on his chair, his hands grasping the arms on either side of him, and this was unusual for Arthur, for most of the time he was relaxed with the enforced relaxation of a man too fat for tension. John was too recently inebriated to understand the significance of this force. He did not recognize it, and if he had he would have been unable to know that it was something generally foreign to Arthur. On the other hand he was not so intoxicated as to miss the significance of what had been said to him. The room was revolving, but not so much as the case itself. And yet as the case revolved every aspect of it seemed clear to him.

Arthur had explained why Merlin had died, how Merlin had died, and John knew that what had been said to him was something beyond his own powers of deduction.

When Arthur heaved himself to his feet and went over to the bureau, John silently reached his glass across. Arthur started to pour and then, seeing that the bottle was empty, reached down for the third bottle.

There are some things one doesn't do if one has any desire to remain sober. One doesn't get drunk, and then force sobriety, and then pour one's self three inches of eighty-six proof Scotch. Arthur, standing above John, holding his still untouched new glass, was a relatively sober man. John, sitting below him, was still a relatively drunken one. There wasn't a hell of a lot that a new drink could do to John. There was a lot that this new one could do to Arthur. Arthur lifted his glass and said, "Here's to crime," and put it to his lips and took a healthy slug. And John lifted his glass and said, "You're God-damn right," and drained off at least three-quarters of his drink.

"You're God-damn right," he repeated. "I'd a hell of a sight rather be drinking to the guy who killed Merlin than to Merlin. I don't like this case. I don't like any part of it. I got to turn it in. In a little while I got to go down the hall and arrest that guy. Do you think I like that?"

Arthur shook his head and said, "No, you don't like it."

John said, "It burns me." And then he stopped and laughed sardonically at his verb. "Yeah, burns me that that guy has to burn for this murder. He had to kill the bastard, and I could cut my throat for having to arrest him."

233

"It's not so bad," said Arthur. "There's something you don't know." Then Arthur lowered his glass and looked into it and saw that he had drunk off just half the quantity he had poured. Somewhere in the back of his mind he realized that what he was about to say he wouldn't have said if he were sober. And yet he was sober, should have been with all that cold water. What Arthur didn't realize was the effect of a new drink on top of such a forced temporary sobriety.

"Got to tell you something," Arthur said. "Don't want you to worry. Joyce won't burn for this. Got it all fixed up."

"Yes?" said John, and his head came up hopefully. "That's good. How?"

Arthur shook his glass at John. "Don't worry. All fixed up. Look. Tell you about it but you mustn't tell a soul. Really off the record. Got it all fixed up so he doesn't get the chair. Ever hear of Gene August?"

John shut his eyes and concentrated on this. "Left something out," he said. "June, August. Left out July."

"Uh-uh," said Arthur. "You're missing the point. Not June. Gene. Gene August, the big lawyer. You know."

"Oh, that guy," said John. "What about him?"

"He's here," said Arthur. "Right here in this hotel. Talked to him today. Fixed it up. He's going to defend Joyce. Got the defense all set. Joyce gets off easy."

"How do you do that?" said John.

"Cinch," said Arthur. "It's the plea. Temporary insanity. Tell you something. Tell you something about June August. Never defended anybody on murder rap who got the chair. Always gets them off. This is set. Can't miss.

234

Especially since Merlin hit Joyce. Very hard blow. Probably deranged him temporarily."

"That's good," said John. "That's very good. Wish you'd kept your big yap shut, though."

"What's the matter?"

"You go telling me about it! I'm the police. I work with the D.A. Right?

"Oh, hell," said Arthur.

"That's right. I work with the D.A. I got to tell him what your plea's going to be. He knows way in advance, maybe he can knock it over."

With the air of a man who knew he had drunk too much and a little more couldn't hurt, Arthur gulped again at his drink.

"Look, kid. Something I've been wanting to tell you. I got a big job here—more than I can handle—running this hotel, handling Merlin's magazine and the books. I don't know whether there will be radio and television or not. Probably will with Lovechild taking it over. I need an assistant business manager, see. How would you like the job?"

"You can't do that," said John. "You can't do that to me. You're bribing me."

"What do you mean, bribing you?"

"You're getting me out of the force, aren't you? Getting me out of it fast. Don't want me telling the D.A. what the defense is going to be."

"Go on, tell him," said Arthur. "If you want to. But you'll be crazy, because you're going to be part of this family, you know."

"Am I?"

"You're going to marry Sandra, aren't you?"

"Well, sure, if she'll have me."

"All right. Turn your case in. Turn it in to the D.A. All the facts. Everything we just figured out. And then resign. You won't have to tell the D.A. what our defense is, then, will you?"

John said, "Not unless I want to. But that's the only reason you're offering me this job. You want to get me in a box where I can't talk to the D.A."

"You're stupid," said Arthur. "Ever occur to you I had a better reason for offering you the job? How much do you make?"

"Thirty-six hundred," said John.

"Thirty-six hundred!" Arthur gave a great alcoholic snort. "Do you think I want my niece Sandra living on thirty-six hundred?"

"Doesn't have to live on it," said John. "Got all that inheritance."

"Think I want you not marrying her because you're not making enough to support her and because you don't want to live on her dough?"

"I don't?" said John.

"Of course not," said Arthur. "You wouldn't do a thing like that."

"Hmmm," said John. "Hell of a spot. What are we going to do?"

"What are we going to do?" said Arthur. "I'll tell you what we're going to do. We're going to get you out of that stinking thirty-six-hundred job. I need a twelve-thousand-a-year assistant, see. It's got to be somebody who'll listen to me. In twenty years you're the only person I've met

236

who'd listen to me. I need you, kid. Are you on? Will you do it for me?"

John struggled up out of the chair and extended his hand. "Art," he said. "Mind if I call you Art?"

"Cer'n'y not," said Arthur.

"Art, there's nothing I wouldn't do for you. Not even this." And they clasped hands and together tottered to the bureau and poured another couple of inches for each of them. Arthur walked away from the bureau and John remained there, one elbow on it, the back of his hand to his chin.

"You know, Art, you're not gonna like this. Maybe you're not doing it to bribe me. That would be bad if you were. But what's almost as bad is what I'm thinking now. You're not doing this because you need me for an assistant. You're doing this for Sandra. You want her husband to have a decent job."

"The hell I am," said Arthur.

"Then why the hell *are* you doing it? Why the hell are you getting me off the police force and into a good job if you're not doing it to bribe me, or else for Sandra's sake?"

"Well, I'll tell you, John. You're not going to believe me, but it's the God's honest truth. I'm doing this for the sake of law enforcement. I've gotten real fond of this town, this St. Petersburg; that's what I'm doing it for. You got to admit getting you off the police force here is the most I could do for a town I got real fond of."

John looked up and said, "Gee, you're right. I hadn't seen it that way. You're on. I'll do it. Do you know what I got to do first?"

"No, what do you got to do first?" said Arthur.

237

"Got to lie down and rest for a minute," said John. "It's been a tough case. Fellow's got to get a little rest."

"You go right ahead," said Arthur. "Take one of the beds." And John took one of the beds. He fell into it. And Arthur stood above him swaying back and forth. And he smiled a great vague smile from ear to ear and, carefully dropping his cigar into a vase of flowers on the table, he staggered onto the other bed. In a moment the two of them were mingling their snores.

That's how Hester found them. She came down the hall, tapped at the door, tapped again and, getting no response, pushed it open and there they were, out like a couple of twin lamps.

She started across to them, as if to do something for them, and then she stopped and she went out of the room again and returned in a few moments, this time with Sandra. And the two women looked down at the two men. And then Hester went to Arthur and loosened his tie and took the comforter from the bottom of the bed and spread it over him. And Sandra loosened John's tie and her fingers strayed along the front of his shirt and lingered there, and she tore them away. And she too spread a comforter over her man and then she bent down and gently kissed his forehead. And John, out in some limbo of alcoholic dreams, stirred with what might have been an accidental response and flung an arm around her shoulder and pulled her down and pressed her mouth to his. And then he let her go and Sandra straightened up and stood beside the bed filled with the joyous knowledge of how good a marriage could be to a man whose unconscious instincts were as sound as that.

238

The world never learns. Thirty-six hours before, it had stirred to the freedom implicit in the bulletins of Merlin's death. Now, in a thousand headlines, in hundreds of radio bulletins, the new Word was spreading—the word of Lovechild. There was a response to that word. It wasn't a response of cheers; it wasn't even a response of any conscious act. But across a continent a great many people, afraid to breathe by themselves, afraid to eat on their own, afraid of their own ability to drink or smoke in moderation, welcomed—although they were not yet conscious of it—the word that there was a new Leader who would guide them and guard them. And, as is always the case with those who most need guardianship, they resented him; but they didn't quite know what they would do if forced to get along without him.

And in Merlin's room on the fourth floor of the Broadstone, Lovechild stood before the window smiling to himself. And he breathed in, and he breathed out, and he bent his knees, and he straightened them. And he lay down on the floor and raised his legs above his head and touched his toes behind, and all was right with the world. Nobody shot him.

Not yet.